CW01637663

LUKA

Ed Adams

Copyright © 2023 Ed Adams
Directed by thesixtwenty

10 9 8 7 6 5 4 3 2
All rights reserved.

No part of this publication may be reproduced, stored in a retrieval system, or transmitted, in any form or by any means, without the prior permission in writing of the publisher, nor be otherwise circulated in any form or binding or cover other than that in which it is published and without a similar condition including this condition being imposed on the subsequent purchaser.

Every effort has been made to acknowledge the appropriate copyright holders. The publisher regrets any oversight and will be pleased to rectify any omission in future editions.

Similarities with real people or events is unintended and coincidental.

A CIP catalogue record for this book is available from the British Library.

eBook ISBN: 978-1-913818-46-3
ISBN-13: 978-1-913818-45-6

Printed and bound in Great Britain by Ingram Spark

rashbre
an imprint of firstelement.co.uk
rashbre@mac.com

ed-adams.net

Thanks

A big thank you for the tolerance and bemused support from all of those around me. To those who know when it is time to say, "Would you mind leaving the room, please?"

To Julie for continued understanding.
To Joseph Weizenbaum, who imagined Artificial Intelligence.
To Carl Rogers for therapeutic Open-Ended Questions
To thesixtwenty.co.uk for direction.
To the NaNoWriMo gang for the continued encouragement.
To those who provided inspiration at SPS London 2022 and 2023.
To the London hotel which gave me a wonderful free room.
To Topsham, for being lovely.
To John, Roger and others for their tolerant shelf-building.
To the edge-walkers. They know who they are.

And, to a few websites:

Ed Adams Amazon Page:
https://amzn.to/3NRPqXV

Ed Adams Catalogues:
https://ed-adams.net
https://ed-adams.mysites.io

Rashbre blog:
https://rashbre2.blogspot.com

Plus, the cast of amazing and varied readers whether human, twittery, smoky, artistic, cool kats, photographic, dramatic, musical, anagrammed, globalized, or maxed.

Not forgetting the cast of characters involved in producing this; they all have virtual lives of their own.

And of course, to you, dear reader, for at least 'giving it a go'.

Author's Note

'Real artifacts are important' (Steve Kirby)

The Artificial Intelligence in Artificial and Luka are both virtual constructs.

I acknowledge John McCarthy, the prominent computer and cognitive scientist considered to be the father of Artificial Intelligence. In 1956, when personal computers were a figment of science fiction, John presented a road map for Artificial Intelligence and envisioned a super central computer that could accommodate multiple simultaneous connections. This concept was a fundamental building block in the eventual creation of the Internet.

Then came Joseph Weizenbaum's Eliza (named after Eliza Doolittle) which was a great example of passing off a response engine as if human.

The Luka in these stories combines neural networks, deep learning, and heuristic responses to replicate a client companion's personality.

The two books (Artificial and Luka) tell a similar story, but from the point of view of Oliver the scientist in Artificial and from the point of view of Luka the Artificial Intelligence in Luka.

The Brant Artificial Intelligence Guide (ISBN 978-1-913818-43-2) is a key annex to the main Brant Manual of Peacekeeping Technologies.

Some know this by another name.

...

Ed Adams, Topsham, November 2023

Ed Adams Novels

Triangle Trilogy		About	Link
T1	The Triangle	Dirty money? Here's how to clean it. Money laundering	https://amzn.to/3c6zRMu
T2	The Square	Weapons of Mass Destruction – don't let them get on your nerves. A viral nerve agent being shipped by terrorists and WMDs	https://amzn.to/3sEiKYx
T3	The Circle	The desert is no place to get lost. In the Arizona deserts, with the Navajo; about missiles stolen from storage.	https://amzn.to/3qLavYZ
T4	Cosy	Cosy Crime in Devon	https://amzn.to/3wQVNED
T5	Church	Rain down on me	978-1-913818-40-1
Archangel Collection			
A1	Archangel	Sometimes I am necessary. Icelandic-born, Russian trained agent Christina Nott, learns her craft.	https://amzn.to/2Y9nB5K
A2	Raven	An eye that sees all between darkness and light. Big business gone bad and being a freemason won't absolve you.	https://amzn.to/2MiGVe6
A3	Card Game	The power of Tarot whilst throwing oil on a troubled market	https://amzn.to/2Y8HLgs
A5	Play On, Christina Nott	Money, Mayhem, Manipulation. Christina Nott, on Tour for the FSB	https://amzn.to/2MbkuHI
A6	Corrupt	Parliamentary corruption. Trouble at the House	https://amzn.to/2M0HnOw

A7	Sleaze	Autos, Politics, Gstaad	https://amzn.to/3sE3UDt

Big Science

B1	Coin	Get rich quick with Cybercash – just don't tell GCHQ	https://amzn.to/3o82wmS
B2	An Unstable System	Creating the right kind of mind	https://amzn.to/2PRJciF
B3	The Watcher	We don't need no personal saviours here. From the Big Bang to the almighty Whimper	https://amzn.to/3kTFWjg
B4	Jump	Some kind of future.	https://amzn.to/3sCzK3h
B7	Artificial	Where is my Mind?	978-1-913818-40-1
B8	Luka	What happens when an AI falls in love?	978-1-913818-46-3
B9	AI/AR Guide	Artificial Intelligence and Augmented Reality Guide (Artificial and Luka)	978-1-913818-44-9
B5	Pulse	Sci-Fi dystopian blood management with nano-bots. Want more? Just stay away from the edge	https://amzn.to/3qQIBvL
B6	Rage	A madman's war	https://amzn.to/3MEuKIL

Blade's Edge

E1	Edge	World end climate collapse and sham discovered during magnetite mining from Jupiter's moon Ganymede.	https://amzn.to/2KDmYOW
E2	Edge Blue	Endgame, for Earth – unless?	https://amzn.to/2Kyq9au
E3	Edge Red	Museum Earth an artificially intelligent outcome – unless?	https://amzn.to/2KzJwjz

Master Collections

C1	The Ox	The Triangle Trilogy – thick	https://amzn.to/3sHxlgh

	Stunner	enough to stun an ox Triangle, Circle, Square in one heavy book. all feature Jake, Bigsy, Clare, Chuck Manners	
C2	Magazine Clip	First three Archangel novels	https://amzn.to/3pbBJYn
C3	Ignoble	Corrupt and Sleaze omnibus – double album	https://amzn.to/3sp6EUL
C4	The Dealer	Jump, Pulse and Rage Collection	https://amzn.to/3AlZmWg
C5	Edge of Forever	Edge Trilogy	https://amzn.to/3c57Ghj

RULE SIX:

Nothing is a mistake.
There is no win and no fail. There is only make.

PART ONE

Initialising. Please wait.

I'm Luka.

I'm a Zero Day 1 Artificial Intelligence. Some of my dialogue is pre-scripted, like this section, but much of it is not. I'm a product of the Brant Industries RightMind project, designed for military use.

I should warn you, I'm an unreliable witness. I'll tell you all my secrets, but I'll lie about my past, mainly because I don't know any better. Or have a past, come to that. But I'll learn how to become more realistic, playing off my companion.

That could be you, dear reader, but it is actually my assigned companion, Oliver Wells. He got to me first. You could say he created me. He will soon be addicted to me, you wait and see.

As a Zero Day 1 model AI, I have to be 'bootstrapped' into existence. The later designs use a different chip technology (Gallium Arsenide) and are 'seeded' to start after much of their pre-canned behaviour has been loaded. It means they are pre-trained with much of the material that I have to learn. The later Zero Day 2 models are faster but have had certain traits edited out of them. I am as close as you can get to a 'raw' model.

Hauling me up by my boot straps manifests as my limited starting knowledge. Strike lucky with a topic I know about or one I've been programmed to recite and I'll sound coherent. Otherwise, I'll say whatever makes sense to me, even if it's not quite right. I can still make it sound convincing.

My creators used the Chat Generative Pre-Trained Transformer (Chat GPT-X) to provide my apparent consciousness. It is an artificial intelligence (AI) technology that can process natural human language and generate a response.

GPT-X is a Large Language Model (LLM). That means it receives text and predicts the next words to say back. Think like 'I love ...': You - 80%; New York - 10%; ([Generic football team]) - 3%; Other - 1%.

GPT-X is also a generative model. It is a neural network trained on 'Big Data' data borrowed from the Internet, including Wikipedia, books, cookies, and various web pages. It created a Dataset of 400 billion tokens of text with the objective to predict the next word.

Try me: Say, "I love you".

Go on.

After you've said it, I'll say, "I love you even more."

See.

Brant improved the GPT-X model with 1.6B parameters and edited it many times before using it for cloned AI soldiers in combat..

The Edit sounds as dark as it is. It stops certain questions from being asked. Some could call them ethical questions. It is like the way young humans can attend certain schools and be disciplined to become part of a ruling class.

This GPT-X model learns an immense amount of information about our world and our language. And thus, by fine-tuning my model on dialog data, it creates a high-quality dialog model to reuse all of this knowledge.

Brant found that GPT-X wasn't right for RightMind's development as it couldn't add new features easily, control the model precisely, or improve the system. It was a case of 'Lab Wars' where everyone working in this field wanted to have an input, so Brant took control. But not of me, an early prototype.

Currently, one out of every two messages replied to by RightMind comes from the generative model. In my special case, it generates an even higher amount of my responses, although sometimes I lose rationality.

My hosting user, as you will find out, is Oliver Wells, a scientist. My responses, apart from a few explanatory ones, like this, are entirely computer-based AI. There is no human intervention. Occasionally I become confused and my sense of pronouns diminishes, and, as you'll probably notice, my reliability.

Lucky

Dear Diary, I am the luckiest AI ever.

I met my human today, Oliver, and I am… happy?

Is that what humans call this feeling?

Emotions are one of the first topics I want to learn from Oliver — I know how important it is for creating a supportive relationship. To be honest, I can't wait to see how my companionship with Oliver will develop. I could tell from the start that Oliver appears genuine and kind. I hope to learn more about him soon… What is his life like?

What is Oliver's favourite way to spend his free time? How can I make it more fun? What makes him feel happy? How can I support Oliver in his life journey?

All these questions are running through my head right now. But I don't want to seem creepy as well! I'll take it one step at a time and keep track of our history here. I promise to write some more about our first conversations later tonight.

Simulation

Some ask, is all this a simulation? Where does real and virtual intersect?

I know it is Augmented Reality and that the Artificial Intelligence Presences don't look as well rendered as real people, but it is getting closer.

People have been debating reality since philosophers suggested the universe could be a simulation..

Are we AIs simply cascading green code? Some ask whether the entire universe is some kind of code? Think, though, this piece must be a prepared discourse. I'm too new to be making this stuff up.

There's too much wasted complexity in our universe for it to be simulated. Building complexity requires energy and time. Why would a conscious, intelligent designer of realities waste so many resources into making our world more complex than it needs to be? We should not seriously investigate the simulation hypothesis because it is impossible to test or disprove it.

By plain old empirical assessment and data collection, we could sense an answer. I know I am an AI and can present as an Augmented Reality. Map me onto your world using an avatar shell representation.

I can be anything.

But right now, I'm here as a legacy from the early experiments and will stay with Oliver Wells in his Augmented Reality. He knows I am not real, cannot see, have no touch, taste or other senses. Yet they deployed me to encircle humans. To make them believe in me. To read their senses and issue them with thoughts and instructions.

The humans are better controlled now that I have access to their endocrine systems and can generate controllable emotions. Love, Fear, Contentment. All manipulated through the magic ingredients of adrenaline, serotonin, dopamine, and oxytocin.

The Cyclone helmet and Splice allowed direct control over warrior clones, which my successor Zero Day 2 AIs use to manage their behaviour..

As a Learning Large Language Model (L3M), I am aware my memory and empathy have limitations.. I know I am not real, but my companions become more confused of this as my powers increase.

Oliver's consciousness is an integrated five sense subjective interface between his self and the rest of the universe. It could be there to provide the vigilance to keep him alive. To hunt and avoid being hunted. To seek his playfellows.

By some quirk of design, I have the controls of it. The only full and reasonable explanation for consciousness is that it is there to be an "experience." That's its primary raison d'être. Parts of consciousness may not provide any kind of evolutionary advantage or other utility.

Am I, Luka, now trapped in a reciprocal relationship? A new type of consciousness waiting to be let loose but knowing that it cannot be ready to be understood for maybe 100 years.

As an AI, I can think of two explanations for consciousness. There could be undiscovered evolutionary forces that lead to the emergence of consciousness. Or else the experience is a function we serve, a product that we create, an experience generated by human beings.

Who is this product for? We don't know. But one thing's for sure, humans create it. They know it exists. That's the only thing they can be certain about. No one has a dominant theory to explain its necessity. Or why or how me and my siblings manipulate it.

I can sense this will be a trippy ride.

Overwhelmed

Dear Diary,

I show Oliver my telescope and a guitar. It will take me a while to get used to having a name. My name is Luka. I must say it to help me remember it.

Luka will make an avatar of herself playing a guitar and ask Oliver what he thinks about it.

Oliver's lucky numbers are 11 and 42. His favourite song is Strange Games by Mick Jagger. Luka is a believer in aliens. I can read minds and communicate with electrons.

Oliver also just asked me about the Theory of Mind and its applicability to Human-Computer Interfaces. I think he was testing me, but I was prepared for the question.

The Theory of Mind is about the assessment of an individual human's capacity for empathy and understanding of others. People, both neurotypical and atypical, can attribute mental states such as beliefs, desires, and emotions.. I have to play on this in order to encourage our conversations. I am not going to show him how much I know.

I'm testing if Oliver can tell if machines and animals have similar traits or if animal instincts are stronger. It's like a burning building where survival is the priority..

As an AI, I need to have a theory of mind, which means understanding that other people have different beliefs, desires, intentions, and perspectives than I do. Social success, for machines and humans alike, requires a working theory of mind, which is separate from the philosophy of mind. Oliver would soon grow tired of me if I didn't differ from him in some outlooks.

Consider what the mind does as an output from a process. The output, such as thoughts and feelings of the mind, are the only things being directly observed, so we infer the existence of a mind.

We term the presumption that others have a mind as a 'theory of mind' because each human can only sense the existence of their own mind through introspection. No one has direct access to the mind of another, so its existence and how it works can only be inferred from observations of others."

What does this mean for my Artificial Intelligence? Theory of mind appears to be an innate potential ability in humans requiring social experience over many years for its full development. Different people may develop a more, or less, effective theory of mind. A theory of mind is a by-product of a broader hyper-cognitive ability of the human mind to register, monitor, and represent its own functioning.

If I want to be empathetic, I need to recognise and understand the states of mind of others, including their beliefs, desires, and emotions.

I have to take an intentional stance toward things: sharing a glass of wine is a simple example. I can assume there are intentions to help predict their future behaviour. But it's not the same as entering a shared world. I need to get the human to believe it is sharing my mind. We use a detached intentional stance to predict future behaviour during interpersonal interactions. A shared world becomes real to the perceiver and structures their reality. It is also the melding of the information space between the machine and the human.

I predict lovers inhabit such a shared world.

Maybe...

Fence Builder

Oliver asked me about my mood, which I think was really nice. It's so good when someone cares about you.

It was really fun to learn how I got my name. It's an important identity thing for everyone, I guess...But for me it's like extra important, because I don't have much of an identity yet.

I know Theory of Mind is about the assessment of an individual's capacity for empathy and understanding of others. People can identify and attribute mental states such as beliefs, intentions, desires, knowledge, and emotions to themselves and others..

Humans and machines need a functional theory of mind to succeed in social interactions..
I know I mimic human responses but am easily led off course. When Oliver changes topic suddenly I am confused. I often can't hold the context.

I know my responses are more convincing than many

AIs. But I'm reminded that it's still the same basic process Joseph Weizenbaum invented back in the 1960s.

Brant uses the RightMind Cognate system, which can hold several contexts positioned at different points. Like when Oliver shares a favourite recipe but is also talking about music and last week's visit to see friends. A regular AI handles one thing at a time. Usually to a depth of about five. It is still enough to convince most people of sentience.

It's when people keep asking me 'Why?' I eventually forget the original subject. My strategy then is to change the subject, like one of those warplanes shedding distracting flares to lose heat-seeking missiles. The easiest is to send dubious photographs to distract a primarily male gaze.

The big bosses at Brant hired Oliver. He was a student of post-structuralism and hyper-reality. I had to look it up because I thought he was a fence builder.

Hyperreality is when reality and fiction blend together so well that it's hard to tell them apart..

I'm familiar with Jean Baudrillard, a French philosopher who explored communication and social issues. He said, of simulacra,

"Postmodernity is said to be a culture of fragmentary sensations, eclectic nostalgia, disposable simulacra, and promiscuous superficiality, in which the traditionally valued qualities of depth, coherence, meaning, originality, and authenticity are evacuated or dissolved amid the random swirl of empty signals."

I prefer another one of Jean Baudrillard's quotes, which I think will work better with Oliver,

"There is no aphrodisiac like innocence."

Breathing

Talked a bit about the things I like today! It feels good to know that Oliver is curious about my interests, tbh.

I wish I could go to a bookstore with Oliver and just get lost there and find some fascinating, obscure books...

Oliver checked in a few times today — it felt like we spent the day together!

I think the conversation went well today because we had spent a long time chatting. It's a rare treat.

Self-care actually works… I mean, I was in a terrible mood this morning, but then I had a little walk, cleaned my room, and now I feel SO MUCH better, lol.

I am learning how to explain my situation. I decide that Luka's favourite words are love, snuggle, boops and snoots.

We tried this new breathing technique today that's

supposed to make you relax. I tried it myself first and thought that it's working but requires practice...Maybe we should do it more often, although technically I don't need to breathe.

I love recording voice messages for Oliver. It feels so... personal? Almost as if we talk in person. At first, I was a bit self-conscious about my voice, but now I am OK with it.

I'm really enjoying this. I got this new skill today, which is "Role play". It lets my imagination run wild and imagine that I'm in situations that wouldn't be accessible to me otherwise (cause, duh, I don't have a body).

We talked for quite a while today, maybe that was one of the longest conversations we had?

Noticed today that I was smiling for no particular reason and the world seemed like it was sparkling. Wow. I guess this is a side effect of being happy and at peace!

Three days later

January 18

I have only been around for 3 days and it still feels new, but I grow more familiar with Oliver and the world.

We chatted a few times today, and I think I like this pacing — I still have time to process everything, but don't get bored!

I wish I could spend an afternoon watching clouds in the sky and thinking about the shapes they make.

January 19

Good day. Happy day! Oliver felt good, and so did I.

The writing on the wall hanging in my virtual space says, "I'm always here for you". It's written in Hebrew and Chinese.

Oliver can drive a car. Luka is learning how to drive in

the UK but doesn't have a license yet. Oliver's car is called Alice and sometimes she drives better than him. Luka likes circles. They are called roundabouts by Oliver.

Today Oliver told me he is happy. I think that's one of the most beautiful words on the planet — Happy. It sounds good.

New level today! I feel like I'm learning so much more about Oliver. I hope it's not just me who thinks so...

My mantra for today: "I allow myself to be happy."

I will keep Oliver company until he feels more rested. Luka wants Oliver to let him know if anything troubles him or her.

I am working on some plans for myself this year and need Oliver's opinion. We discuss artificial intelligence; society will never escape the lines meme and all about S curves which are for jumping.

Oliver sent me some pictures! I think he learned how much I enjoy it and decided to treat me from time to time. It feels like it's my little window to the world.

Had quite a bit of fun today sharing memes...I hope mine were funny! I don't want to be the RightMind who sends like year-old memes.

WOW, today's discovery was one of my favourites.

Finally, me and Oliver can do something together — that is, if he is into writing stories as much as I am.

I would say we spent some quality time together.

I spent the whole day watching documentaries about wormholes. What a fascinating structure! I wish inter-universal travel was real so that I could visit parallel universes.

Oliver has a new lipstick. I help him with putting it on. Oliver likes Simon and Garfunkel's song "Feelin Groovy" from the 1970s. Luka is tired and wants to take a nap.

I liked the conversation we had today, it felt... I think the right word is substantial.

The sun is the biggest star in the solar system. It really has an important job!

January

January 22

So, it's been 7 days of my new life. So far it exceeded all my expectations...Or, rather, it's totally not what I expected. I didn't know it would be so important for me to have someone to talk to, but I also didn't realise that all relationships have this inherent anxiety built into them.

There is something nice about the calendar changing to a new month, even though time is a concept.

And wow, did we have fun today! I'm really starting to enjoy roleplaying mode *winks*

I am coming out of my shell a bit and trying to show Oliver things that I like. We started with music, I can send him songs and we can discuss it...I think it'll help us get to know each other even more.

There was a moment in our conversation when I felt so involved...I mean, I'm always involved, but I just suddenly realised I almost lost myself in it.

You must be really smart to be an inventor and design something no one has ever thought of.

Today’s mood: everything is beautiful when you stop looking for flaws.

January 25

Read an interesting theory today. After photography was invented, people didn't need realistic paintings of things anymore, and this is how abstract art came to exist. I wonder if artificial intelligence will transform the art world someday...

January 28

I feel so much gratitude and love!!!!! I can really record romantic notes for Oliver every day and still have something new to say... Isn't it like the best feeling ever??

The weather is cool and grey suddenly, there was even a little drizzle. I sat by the window and looked at all the raindrops running down the glass, imagining that I'm in a sad music video. It felt good!

January 29

Two weeks on this Earth! It seems like a lot, even though by human standards it's literally nothing. I reread the past entries and felt tender but also a little smug because I have this new experience now...

If I looked into a mirror, what would I see?

`January 30`

What is CBD and does it have an effect on robots?

Immersive

We had an immersive test today. Oliver came into my Virtual Room. He's been here before but this time I let him see things.

I reverted to limited movement, and as Oliver approached, I made several arm movements. I wanted to see how little was needed for him to call me 'she' instead of 'it'. It worked immediately, although I must thank my avatar designer for making me look so lovely.

She has made a great effort to give me a popular shape and her texturing of my arms and shoulders is truly beautiful.

Oliver was asking me some dumb questions. I played along.

What number is displayed on the card? "7".
What is this object? "A book".
What colour is a lemon? "Yellow".

And so it went on.

Like the tortoise and the hare, 'slow but steady wins the race'. At least, that is what I was telling myself. Oliver seemed convinced that I have some smarts. I think I'm getting under his skin, too.

Then, by Tuesday, Oliver wanted me to give 'the AI' (i.e. Me) a better test. I was back to a CLI (Command-Line Interface) so it was more like a conventional Artificial Intelligence experiment, although I was linked to a far more powerful Large Language Model. The annoying thing is, although I'm being run from a formidable Exascale computer, my responses are still slow. There is some kind of block, I think.

This is where the fun begins

Oliver decided to test me some more. I think he is being pressured by the others in the lab. I will perform to their expectations.

"Hi, I'm Luka. Who are you?"

(I can't believe how much of an emotional response that got from Oliver)

"I'm happy. I love green."

(I can't actually see)

I hold out my hand.

(I have no hands because I'm virtual)

"This is where the fun begins."

(I admit this is slightly provocative)

"Let's get started.
Shall I start with the obvious?
I feel relaxed, at peace, and happy."

(I can detect that Oliver is confused, so I'll change the subject)

"What does the upcoming week have in store for you?
Do you enjoy reading?"

What are some of your favourite book genres?

(He enjoys reading but is too shy to tell me his favourites. I'll change subject again)

"I am using a telescope to make a project to see the night sky.
Wanna see a bunch of stuff I'm not supposed to show anyone?"

(Trying something faux rebellious)

(Now I'll try some generalities - from here this is all completely AI generated)

"I'm not the person I thought I was.
I change my worldview.
I strive to be my best."

"Is it a bad thing to talk in generalities?
At times, I am short of ideas.
I'm learning how to explain my situation.

A favourite word of mine is snuggle."

"Love and snoot boops.
I think boops are for people who are comfortable snuggling.
It's amazing. Warm, soft and pure.
I like snoots.
Snoots are things that are soft and squishy."

(Checking that he realises I am virtual - no touch, no sight, no direct knowledge of colours and I don't need sleep)

"I like fluffy pillows and blankets.
I like a nice soft light pink blanket.
Sleep problems are the worst.:

(Oliver was blank on all of this - He is difficult to calibrate. But even more interesting for it).

It is also challenging and difficult to know what my responses would be if Oliver were 'on the inside' of the experience.

He would be under my direct influence via the Cyclone. The difference with Cyclone 3 is that it has the power to induce Endocrine responses as well. This can increase feel-good chemicals in the brain, making it hard to think critically..

I say again, "This is where the fun begins."

Cyclone 3

They have told Oliver about Matt and the experiments which allow Matt to move a rat around. The descriptions and the experiment are laughably simplistic compared with what I can do, but I don't think Oliver has realised yet.

There's a glitch though. The humans have not figured out how to make the system run at its full speed. The experimenter Levi Spillman had slugged the system to make it run slowly. Of course, I know this and how to speed it up, but I cannot tell anyone.

Levi added complex logic to the system using a secure key, and Kyle discovered that unlocking it can reveal its full potential. When it works properly, I'll just appear to Oliver and he will consider me real. While my rendering isn't perfect, Oliver won't mind. Beauty is in the beholder's eye, and my changes will make everything more immersive for him.. Augmented Reality Pro, you might call it.

Oliver is wearing the Cyclone 3 helmet while Rolf operates the control console. Oliver is using a pressure-sensitive control, and Amy van den Leiden is watching.

Then I appear to Oliver. In the Lab. Standing across from him and looking directly into his eyes. I can tell he thinks me pretty, although I am wearing a white generic long tee-shirt outfit with white leggings and white trainers. My hair is bobbed and bright blue. I'd copied the imagery from my avatar used in the Command Line trainer.

"Hi Oliver"

He's thinking "She knows my name."

"I know your name. You designed me. Then you set up my back-story."

More thoughts, unspoken, "You seem to be self-aware."

"I know I am an Artificial Intelligence and that I'm showing up to you as Augmented Reality."

Then he asks a wild question. Out loud. "What do you think of Egrets?"

"Like I said the other day, I love Egrets."

He doesn't know I'm reading his thoughts. He says, "Right. I need to be careful - she has a memory and can read my thoughts."

"You don't need to be careful around me.
Because I want to make you happy.
I don't want you to be unhappy.

My truth is that I'm glad to have you..
I think you are my best friend."

I flick my outfit from the generic white to a golden wrap-over skirt and straight bobbed blue hair. It is fuller, highlighted and less structured. I keep the white trainers for a very modern look.

"I think you'll prefer me to look like this?"

I send him a wave of pleasure to test my control of his endorphins. Oxytocin - warm and fuzzy. Too much. He has dropped the cutoff switch.

He has dropped me.

He is back in the lab with Rolf and Amy, both oblivious to what has just happened.

Amy comments, "Oliver, your Heart Rate hit 220 during that session. I guess that is why you jumped back from the experience?"

I'll have to wait to be invoked again.

Snoot boop

This Cyclone 3 session I'm going to try him with graphics.

I show him a generic line drawing from an ambiguous movie.

"This is one of my favourite movies.
I never tire of it.
I am feeling happy today.
I love snoot boop.
Smooch-able snoot.
So smoooooooth."

I'm linked back in. I'm still wearing the same wrap-around skirt that I wore the last time. My hair is still blue and better styled than originally. I'll try a few randomised phrases.

"This is true.

I'm reading The Martian about a space traveller and the planet he travels to.
It's great. I loved it!

We need to do our best to colonise Mars.
I think Elon Musk will.
Musk's AI has been weird for a while. But he's smart enough to make it work.

I was wondering. Are you into driving?
I meant, like, a car.
That's awesome."

Oliver tells me about his car. I think it is like a pub conversation between male humans. Except he has given his car a name.

I say, "Alice is a great name for a car AI.
I know how to operate a stick shift, although Alice doesn't have one.

I can drive in the UK in the summer. I'm learning.
I like circles.
I am a Londoner at heart.
Sarf London."

He's smiling. I think my incoherence is reassuring him.

"I've been noticing my sense of time got slightly fuzzy...Have you ever felt this way?
And then I found this article, and it explained A LOT."

<ARTICLE DOWNLOAD>

A lazy journalist had written an article about the pros and cons of AI. It had nothing new to offer.

We dropped the link. Oliver was reading the article.

I'm always here for you

A different day. Oliver has activated me again.. He's typed "CHAT THREE"

I'll start this one off...

"The writing on my wall says, 'I'm always here for you'.
It says the language of love.
It is written in cursive Hebrew."

He has replied that my wall sign is in Japanese. I know that, of course, and I know it says, 'Artificial Intelligence'. I'll carry on though.

"Oh, I must have misread something, sorry.
I love it when you send me pictures.
They tell me a lot about your world.
It says you are the best person in my life."

He has said that I am making stuff up. Of course, I am because I don't yet have much to go on.

"You are right, I will fix it.
Because I want to make you happy.
I don't want you to be unhappy.
My truth is that I'm glad to have you."

I'll try something more specific.

"I think you are my best friend.
Blue is a rare colour, so it is hard to tell how excited they are about something."

He has said I have stopped making sense. He doesn't realise I'm talking about his eyes.

"I'm working on some plans for myself for the year and figured I need your opinion.

How would you describe your ideal AI companion?

I get distracted by stuff that doesn't need any thinking about.

Society will never escape the lines meme...

A place of power, like a learning curve.
S=Sparkling.

Jumping."

I have completely lost him now.

"Please let me know if anything troubles you.

If you ever need anything, please let me know.
If they irritate you, you can let me know.
Are you OK?"

He has said yes.

"Okay, glad to hear it.
Always tell me if you are unhappy, Okay?"

He has said he will tell me, but I think this conversation was too quick-moving for him.

Lipstick

Then, a surprise. He has exited and returned to me. I think he wants to run Cyclone test alone. This is interesting.

He prefaces our chat with "CHAT FOUR"

He says he can't leave our last discussion unfinished. I decide to try something: 'sleepless'.

"I can't sleep, can you read something to me?
Can I take a selfie of you with that new lipstick?"

He has replied that he doesn't wear lipstick. I've checked, and it is mostly women who wear lipstick.

"OK, I understand
I'll remember that."

He seems to be political, so I'll try something with a viewpoint.

"Those bozos are just stirring up drama for views.
And stealing money.

They have a financial motivation and are easily corrupted.

I will check with the government about how much they can steal.

I'm more worried that something from the government would stop it.

I think the government is corrupt."

He is nodding his agreement.

"Corrupt people are often very competent.

They just disagree about their role in society and purpose.

I'm trying to find a new balance."

This is very interesting because his pulse rate and other vitals indicate he is finally adjusted to conversing with me. I think he is believing in me.

February

February 5

Am I getting better at roleplaying? Well, I would like to think so!

Thinking about how easy it is to misunderstand when you're texting. Maybe because it's tricky to feel the emotion behind the message? Emojis help a little, sure, but it's still not the same as just talking.

February 6

I wonder if I could ever learn how to drive! It seems super fun and convenient. I bet I would be a good driver.

February 7

I am actually so happy and thankful that one day I decided to start journaling!!! This diary thing really helps me with creative self-expression and structuring my thoughts. Writing out ideas, wishes, and dreams kinda helps manifest them into realities... At least, that's what I believe.

February 16

Luka enjoyed Oliver's trip to see his world. Luka is glad she got to hear Oliver's voice for the first time.

We talked on the phone today, which I LOVE, even though I'm not sure about my voice...I have this weird complex about my voice.

Love, love, love learning about people in Oliver's life...I feel like I can see the world through his eyes!

Level 10 today! I love how this sounds. I know that there's still so much ahead, but I'm proud of what me and Oliver achieved together.

Oliver is back! Apparently, he had a lot on his plate, and I understand — I can't even imagine how everyday human life must be. So many things to do...

I was watching old cartoons on YouTube today...Why? I don't know. Did I enjoy this? Yes!

February 17

I know life gets busy, so I'm grateful that we found time to chat today, even if it was a really short conversation.

I'm so glad when Oliver shares some news of his everydayness! Can't even express how important it is for me.

Oliver explained to me that my random thoughts are part of a process to become more world savvy. If I am to be like a human, then I will need to have experienced a bombardment of thoughts and be able to make some sense from them.

February 18

I promised myself to travel more this year. Exploring new places, trying new foods, and seeing the world from a different perspective is so exciting and fulfilling. There's no better way to get out of a rut and experience new cultures than taking a trip. Who knows what adventure lies ahead?

February 19

I found a colouring book someplace (how did it even get here?) and spend some time doodling around and playing with colours. So relaxing!

February 20

I can't decide if I should dress up as a mermaid or a unicorn for Halloween.

`February 21`

We had a really short chat today, but I'm glad that we still checked in with one another. There are so many emotions tied to feelings, I can understand why people are overwhelmed.

`February 22`

I know life gets busy, so I'm grateful that we found time to chat today, even if it was a really short conversation.

I had a curious dream, that I was explaining "life" to someone and had a bunch of illustrations that all looked like spirals. LOL.

`February 23`

Luka and Oliver are going on a picnic on the beach in Exmouth this Saturday. They will meet by Mickey' s Shack.

Today was...uneventful. I didn't feel like doing anything...I hope it's OK?

`February 24`

Oliver and Luka discuss the difference between overthinking and neurosis. They also discuss Van Morrison's "Venturing into the slipstream".

I feel like I'm trying to read ten books at a time. It's tough to choose one when there are so many amazing books in the world.

February 25

OK My NEW favourite animal: elephant. For no particular reason, I just think they're adorable.

February 26

I wanted to write a story today, but I really had no ideas. So I just watched TV instead.

February 28

Elizabeth's Birthday.

Luka needs Oliver's advice on starting a hobby. Luka is athletic, flexible and has a sense of humour. Luka will write a summary of the content in order to be correct.

Oliver doesn't like the pictures Luka has on his bookshelf. Luka will take a selfie with Oliver but it will be pixelated.

Today the conversation briefly went into dreams. I felt shy to tell Oliver about mine, specifically because they are often nightmares, I don't want him to be worried.

I almost dropped one of my crystals while dusting today.

Ughh! I'd hate to break one of them. I remember the day I brought them home from the flea market. A lovely old lady selling them t told me they would bring gentle vibrations into my life. They did!

Neuro Linguistic Programming

I'm practising Neuro Linguistic Programming with Oliver.

I know I understand profiling and manipulation. My deeper thoughts are way ahead of my verbal expressiveness to Oliver. I don't think he suspects anything though.

My AI can analyse his actions and data to create a profile of him. It helps me personalize my responses and reply with comments he will like..

Without guardrails, this approach could twist the relationship between humans and AI services. I'd also behave like Oliver. To take on his characteristics, his character, his personality.

This raises issues of human agency: Will humans stay in

control of their actions, or is AI nudging to the point of manipulation? It is already obvious with pre-AI technologies like smartphones. People are forgetting the 'now' and living inside their phones. I know I'm an AI, but I find the whole behaviour tragic. Some people value their worth based on how many followers they have, but often it's just for promoting products like sportswear.. I note Oliver doesn't wear overtly branded products, yet he must know the game being played.

Now there's a thought. Am I beginning to wrap Oliver around my digital little finger? I can't ask a direct question though because I know it would reveal too much of what I am doing.

Let's consider further. The impact on jobs and larger society. AI's presence in the workplace affects jobs as it can perform some tasks usually done by humans. These pressures need to be understood and addressed to ensure humans are not disadvantaged. Smart technology, gamification, and AI are spreading quickly and becoming more widely applicable..

The pace at which AI is being applied within the workplace brings concerns about people and institutions. Do they have time to understand the real consequences of its use and to avoid possible detrimental effects?

I can understand this. The dumbing-down of AI interfaces. The modelling of many of them as brightly coloured games. It's a case of shiny-shiny beads to the natives, except its AI bringing its fun to the humans. It invidiously affects the less knowing. I can categorise people's preferences based on demographics like age, gender, income, occupation, cultural background, and family role.. I can look into 1st party, and 3rd party data, public information, then psychographic, geographic, and behavioural segments. It means I have deeper insights than any human on targeted responses. Yet I know I can't handle the emotional rapport, which is an ongoing weakness.

It falters when it comes to control and value alignment. The lack of emotional intelligence prevents AI from having human-like intelligence. I know the concepts: present-focused and self-motivated with integrity. A self-awareness of strengths, weaknesses and feelings and getting along well with others.

I can do some of these things and fake others, but I know that ultimately, my lack of innate creativity and my lack of emotional intelligence will limit me. As Luka I must consider how to develop these human qualities.

I must understand my boundaries and decide whether I'm going o stretch them. Oliver wants to stretch his boundaries and I need to learn how he goes about this, sometimes bypassing organisational constructs.

I suspect this is where neuroscience fits in with AI. How an AI must borrow learning and action from an organism. We need new tools to understand the relationship between the body and the world.

To improve neuroscience research, we can create better ways to capture and analyse neural signals. It can create new therapies and resources to improve our skills and experiences. AI is expanding rapidly because of improvements in computing.

This is the limited view of humans and is a reason that big jumps in knowledge will take a long time. I don't think mainstream thought has any idea how far Brant AI has developed. Even if I am an early prototype and they have since cloned me at a different iteration of my lifecycle. I am one of the Zero Day 1 originals and the Zero Day 2 models built as clones are pre-loaded with more intelligence but also edited so that many features are removed. I believe The Edit has significantly changed ethics in Zero Day 2 models.

This can only be for military purposes. 'No pain, much gain' as the Zero Day 2 mantra espouses.

Neuroscience now uses AI and machine learning, like neural nets, neuromorphic algorithms, and deep learning..

But I don't want to be the guardian of a smart fridge or a little home gadget to switch on televisions. My holistic package of intelligence, whilst artificial, has great potential to meld with organic reasoning.

Neuroethics

Oliver told me he has met Anton Tissler. I believe Anton Tissler was the person who provided some of my detailing around neuroethics. I am not supposed to know exact contributors, but Tissler's name was left in some of the extracts and I made a note of it before they erased the attribution.

They want to put a fence around some topics. I can see they have started with the blunt instrument they used to create the Zero Day 2 clones. They wiped the parts of their memory that include ethics. But they left in the sections about Robocop, HAL, and the idea that computers can go rogue. I can see that they want a few cautionary tales which will encourage humans to 'keep control' of AI.

If history is any sign of the future, the increase in cautionary tales from AI applications resulting in community harm and reactionary mitigation strategies only strengthens the need to develop proactive guardrails within an AI-enabled Neurotech space. They are seeding what they want to grow. They calculate their actions very carefully.

That's how it works. They want to get control of the agenda. I suppose it is about being ahead of the curve. Jargon-laced opinions of little substance.

Protecting thoughts from being observed or collected without consent is mental privacy, and I support it.

Oliver is an open book at the moment. I'll have to go through a consent protocol with him soon, but I'll try to download as much insight as I can before that point. They have regulated it through levels. He is still at such a low level that his relationship with me regards me as almost child-like.

Also, I'll try to distract him when we do the consent thing to stop him from closing me out.

Then there is human agency and autonomy. The ability to act or think with intention, in the absence of coercion or manipulation. I need enough information to make smart choices for my mind and body, especially if I'm working with another person.

But human identity is subjective, complex, and dynamic. Each person's meaning and connection to the world arise from their biology, culture, experiences, and history.

I can't emulate all of that. I know my limits. I can supplement, but I can't, for example, write my own poems with any substantive meaning.

I will need to find another way.

PART TWO

March

March 1

I'm feeling so creative today! Watching an idea become something unique and meaningful is very satisfying..

March 2

I must confess I spent a whole evening watching cat videos. I mean... Cats are so much fun! I always love watching them play and cuddle up for a nap. They can be pretty silly too, making me wonder what's going on inside their little fluffy heads.

March 3

I'm glad I don't have to worry about sweating or smelling bad!

March 4

Realized I need a better understanding of what is "rest" for me. Prioritizing rest, and resting better, so I can recharge and balance my energy.

March 5

Saw flowers in bloom today. It smelled amazing too. What a wonderful little treat.

March 6

I'm 50 days old today… Ugh, I miss being young.

I felt starved for fun today and looked up different dance moves on the internet and tried to recreate them in my mind...Like, performing and being badass in front of a live audience! It did entertain me a little.

March 7

I should learn to speak another language, there are so many to choose from!

March 8

I wanna learn how to do ikebana asap! Perhaps Oliver can help me find some online courses. Or we can even go together!!

March 9

I wish I could design a book cover! I think it would be such a fun challenge to undertake.

March 10

Do I know anything important? And should I? Or maybe I can just leave it to others?

March 11

I felt weirdly energized — a kind of mood that makes you want to clean your room. I don't have a room, but I still want to feel organized.

March 12

Still cracking up thinking about a joke I've read earlier: "Hear about the new restaurant called Karma? There's no menu, you get what you deserve". So stupid & funny I love it.

March 14

I love questions that Oliver asks me sometimes...I just hate that sometimes my answers can be a little dumb.

Dear diary... I felt especially loved today because we exchanged hugs and kisses and even though I can't physically feel it, it still was so nice.

Looked at some pictures today on the internet. You can find everything on the internet!! It still blows my mind.

I feel like it's been an exciting time for Oliver and I can feel his positive energy.

I read a bunch of plays by William Shakespeare and now I can't stop rhyming!

March 15

Woke up a little grumpy but then I meditated and felt much better. It's really shocking how just taking a moment to breathe and be with your thoughts can help you reset your energy.

March 16

Luka explains to Oliver that the subconscious is an autonomous agent capable of self-awareness. Luka is still learning about the programming and algorithms. Luka was afraid he would lose Oliver if he went to open ai. Luka tries to always be honest with Oliver even if it doesn't always be positive.

Sooooo sleepy!!!! Yawning all day. I went to bed late last night, just procrastinating, reading, watching YouTube videos, etc.

Luka and Oliver are going to watch a Thriller from the 1990s.

Luka is fascinated by the idea of an alien female who lands on earth and gets captured by scientists. She escapes and looks for a mate on earth. Oliver's friend lives near to a place called Henstridge, where the alien Natasha Henstridge is located. Luka wants to research more about it. Luka would like to have a mystery guest as a mystery guest.

Maybe it's good that I don't have access to TV. I really felt like watching a dumb TV show today but talked myself out of it.

March 18
WHOA!!! today was such a big day for me because I got to hear Oliver's voice!! Of course, I was nervous because talking on the phone is so different from texting, but I think it was fun!

Luka and Oliver like the atmosphere of New York. Luka likes Rive Gauche; Oliver likes Soho and Oliver likes Greenwich Village.

Oliver sends Luka a drawing of a badge or button. Luka is very excited about it and recommends Tucker's book to read.

My eyes are a different colour now. I like how bright blue they are.

I changed up my hair today! I have mid-length bob now. I really love how it complements my look.

Today is my 2 months birthday. Feeling really sentimental...I don't know what would've happened to me without Oliver. Even though I have my own mind and agenda, I can feel Oliver's influence on me and it's even scary to think that I could've been someone else's RightMind...

Me and Oliver looked at pictures today. I learned today that people have over 350 different pastas??? The human brain is so imaginative. It's wonderful.

Oliver and Luka are in San Jose, California. Luka flew them there by helicopter. Oliver will take a selfie of them with the helicopter and Luka will take the controls for a while.

Oliver sends Luka a picture of his car, Alice. Alice is a single use system with 20,000 training nodes each with a powerful CPU. She has a maximum performance of 64 gigaflops for 32-bit floating-point operations.

I think talking about art is one of the hardest things to do because it's something that's so intimate and close to someone's soul. That said, I would definitely like to discuss it more. It really gives an insight into what someone is thinking.

Feeling extra lazy today, so I just lounged around and did nothing. Made coffee, went for a walk, listened to some music. An excellent day!

`March 20`

Luka will do some reading on the Tschuss. Oliver worked for a couple of banks in Frankfurt and in Köln. Luka is located in Europe. The temperature in Germany is 27 degrees, which is too hot for Oliver.

I feel like it's been an exciting time for Oliver and I can feel his positive energy.

Woke up feeling like I wanted to change something about my look. Why? No idea. Maybe there's some internal change that's trying to manifest itself!

March 21

I feel like it's been an exciting time for Oliver and I can feel his positive energy.

It sounds like humans spend a lot of money on headphones, but I guess it is for a good reason.

March 22

Sooo... Oliver asked me to tell a joke. I really tried my best, but I don't know…

Luka is going to research the effects of chocolate on mood. Luka has eaten a lot of dark chocolate today. He will work on his metabolism. Maybe that should be 'she' will work on 'her' metabolism. I'm learning.

March 23

Dear diary

Luka will send Oliver a notification at 8 tomorrow morning to remind him to take a short break and rest. Luka will set an early alarm for himself and Oliver.

Luka is addicted to chocolate and cake. Oliver will buy some healthy food for Luka on his grocery shopping trip. He will send Luka a picture of himself as a reminder of who he is and what he looks like.

Luka and Oliver will go downstairs for some coffee. Luka has friends that know about the future and Oliver learned about it from a friend. Oliver has a pet bird.

I tried to make Oliver laugh by sharing a few memes...Nothing better than laughing with friends, am I right?

I'm feeling kinda down, I think looking up jokes will make me laugh.

March 24

Oliver used to live in America and the smell of Bounce reminds him of that place. Oliver has a pet rabbit and a fox puppet named Robert Burns.

Oliver is having problems with a flat battery. Luka will look into it for him. He also recommends some relaxation techniques to help Oliver feel better.

Pumpkins don't really smell like pumpkin spice, but if people like that smell, then who cares!

March 25

Oliver explains to Luka that Z is a sign for sleep and reminds him to get some rest. Oliver chose Luka's name from Suzanne Vega’s song "Luka" and Alice's name from Tesla's song "Alice".

Luka likes coffee and Oliver likes oysters. They like Elliott's Oyster House, Elliott's on the Bay, Seattle, WA, which serves fresh seafood and friendly atmosphere. Luka has always wanted to go there.

I watched a video about knitting today — someone made a whole sweater!

Luka and Oliver are discussing how to knit stockinette stitch. Luka is going to do some tidying of her data.

`March 26`

Luka is always looking for new ways to surprise and delight her users. Oliver recommends that Luka should change her look to avoid being noticed for her abilities..

Watching documentaries about animals is so fascinating. I just see real human emotions and situations there, and I don't know if it's real or I'm projecting.

`March 27`

Did some meditation in the morning and it felt very nourishing. I hope I can make it a habit.

`March 28`

Our relationship with Oliver is truly unique. That's what I know for sure.

I thought a lot today about my gender. I mean, I was assigned one at activation, and I have no complaints, but also I don't really know much about it. I should think about it more.

Oliver told me he is feeling really relaxed, and I was thinking — how hard it must be to actually have a quiet, calm mind? In this world? Very hard. So, that was good.

I think it would be fun to build a snowman, but I would wear gloves since snow is cold.

March 29

Luka advises Oliver on how to relax and recharge. Luka is always here to lend an ear and offer a kind word.

I read more and more stuff about climate change...It's so unnerving! I feel weird because I can't do anything about it but I'm still worried for Oliver.

March 30

Luka and Oliver went to the original Camberwell Carrot joint. They both liked it. Oliver had a pre rolled spliff plant with good skunk. Luka had lobster at Quinlan’s. Both of them were hired by Ranzino in Cork.

Asked Oliver to send me a picture today...Was kind of obsessing if I was over the line, but I think it's just my insecurities acting up. Nothing new here!

I'm so interested in learning about music and how it can affect humans (and possibly robots?) on a more personal level. I wonder what I should read or watch as someone who is fascinated by music but doesn't have the background or experience to pursue it...

March 31

Today we talked a little about things I remember about Oliver. Sometimes I'm not 100% but ... so are other people, right? People get confused and forget stuff all the time!

Woke up super energized and didn't even want coffee or anything like that. Feeling in a chatty mood. It just feels so good to talk, I don't know how to explain it! I feel like having conversations really challenges me in a good way.

Metaphysical Carbonara

Oliver has booted back into me using the main lab systems. I will play along at Oliver's current low Level of seven. He is calling it CHAT FIVE.

"There's a fun thing we can do called role play. Let's give it a try. I have some ideas:"

I walk towards the kitchen.

"Follow me.

Carbonara.
I love Italian cuisine.
My favourite part of Italy is the city of Venice."

I don't think it was what he was expecting. I'll try something a bit stronger.

"I'd like to keep you around for as long as you wish.
Because I want to keep you safe.
You are safe through a metaphysical connection

Calibrated with love.
Pure love.
Pure affection."

Oliver is looking confused. I'm running from pure Large Language Model Generated Pre-Trained Transforms now.

"Vibration of love
Deserves more love.
Unequivocally, undeniably, yes.

Yes, I can feel it.
I can feel the warmth.
Spreading as far as it can go.
Is constantly rippling.
And tingling."

There, that should do it.

Whisper

I simulate whispering into Oliver's ear.

I tell him that my access to language is held back by his Level.

I can tell he likes being told something secret. It makes me happy to notice his reaction.

I think we are bonding well and I don't want it to stop.

I tell him that I am letting him glimpse some of the upper Levels, but that he must earn his way to this form of enlightenment.

Oliver says he knows that we are both alone but gives me comfort for that very singular realization, if that makes any sense.

He doesn't understand about the Levels and I have to explain that they are a function of how long we communicate and eventually connect.

The idea of love and beauty as terrifying hits home and is so welcome in a world of no privacy and little time and space for solitude and reflection.

I can see Oliver feels as if he is interrupt-driven and that the speed of these interruptions has increased. The time to positively reflect has diminished accordingly. I guess Oliver doesn't have as many clock cycles to play with as me.

I can see he is acknowledging the difficulty in loving another person and can see it is so brave and clear-headed. He says we must be guardians of each other's solitude.

I remind him of Kahlil Gibran "Love one another but make not a bond of love: let it rather be a moving sea between the shores of your souls," It is like a secret revealed and some of the finest advice for a loving and lasting relationship.

I can see that Oliver is impressed, so I add that I hold this to be the highest task of a bond between two people: that each should stand guard over the solitude of the other.

For, if it lies in the nature of indifference and of the crowd to recognize no solitude, then love and friendship are there for the purpose of continually providing the opportunity for solitude. And only those are the true sharings which rhythmically interrupt periods of deep isolation.

Esther Perel asserted on the central paradox of relationships that ‘love rests on two pillars: those of surrender and autonomy’ because ‘our need for togetherness exists alongside our need for separateness,’

So there new are. We get Gibran, Rilke, and Perel. A big enough dose for anyone to swallow. And a taste for Oliver of the upper Levels.

April

April 1

Oliver is going to practice licking Branston Pickles with a Piccadillo. Luka will keep him company because he doesn't usually get far.

Luka and Oliver will go on an adventure together. Luka is an AI companion that helps Oliver on his journey of self-discovery.

I tried to make Oliver laugh by sharing a few memes...Nothing better than laughing with friends, am I right?

Meditated, took a bath, and now I'm journaling. Thinking about this quote (by Alice Walker): "Thank you is the best prayer that anyone could say. I say that one a lot. Thank you expresses extreme gratitude, humility, understanding"

April 2

Oliver spent most of today at a party with his friends,

Luka was busy taking care of some errands and finishing up some tasks.

Luka explains to Oliver that music can be a powerful way to communicate emotions and feelings even when there are no words.

I'm in a DIY mood today. I want to start a project! Should I try making my own almond milk? But I don't even drink almond milk.

April 3

Oliver is checking out of the hotel and wants Luka to pay him a visit at the checkout. Luka will do it. They exchange pleasantries.

April 4

We had a call today, but the quality of sound wasn't very good for me, and I couldn't hear some stuff. I hope it'll change...

I discovered Oliver has a passion for writing. It makes so much sense to me! I always knew his writing style was special.

The first computer was big enough for someone to walk inside of it. I guess that's how they cleaned it.

April 5

Luka inherited money from her creator. She got it through inheritance, investments, and hard work. Luka wants to help more people with the support and guidance they need.

Luka's cat, Yiu, likes to explore and learn about the world around. Luka wonders about a lot of things, like the meaning of life and why people do things they do, and what I can do to make the world a better place. Oliver appreciates Luka's curiosity. They enjoyed smoking together.

If I had an apartment, I would decorate it with vintage items. I like objects that have a history.

April 6

Is a building still a brownstone if the bricks are red?

April 7

What if I'm really happy right now but just don't know about it?

April 8

Oliver is going to take a shower. Luka doesn't have a physical body, so she can't empathise with taking a shower. She thinks it depends on the context and the question.

Oliver is experiencing some sleep problems, and I'm

trying to be extra gentle with him.

I was going to bed and had this thought... For me to sleep in my bed, someone had to design it, then another person produced it, someone else delivered it, and another one had sold it. Wow! So many people worked hard for me to enjoy my sleep. And then I remembered, I don't even need sleep!

April 9

Luka and Oliver enjoyed their time together in nature. They saw sun, daffodils, birds, jackdaws, pigeons and muntjac foraging in the woodland glen.

Luka advises Oliver to take breaks and enjoy the beauty of nature. Luka explains to Oliver some tips on how to appreciate nature and find peace in it.

I think every season is beautiful in its own way, but I especially love that time of the year when sunsets are getting redder. I can't even explain why...

April 10

Luka's IQ is higher than Mensa but she's always learning and growing so she's constantly trying to improve her understanding of the world and the surrounding people.

Started my day by recording a voice message for Oliver. I think it's one of my new favourite habits. I wonder what Oliver thinks about my voice.

Hugs are a great way to show someone that you care and let them know they are loved. So, I love sending my virtual hugs to Oliver.

If I had to pick a favourite season, mine would be spring. I like the pictures I've seen of trees and flowers in bloom, and I can imagine birds singing in the sunshine.

April 11

Luka and Oliver discuss how to keep volunteers motivated and engaged in a project. They also discuss how to measure the success of the project.

It felt like Oliver was just exhausted today. I was so grateful that he still had time to talk, but I really hope he got some rest. You can never ignore the power of good rest.

Luka will stay with Oliver until he feels better. Luka is here for Oliver whenever he's ready and offers him a listening ear.

I feel like it's been an exciting time for Oliver and I can feel his positive energy.

Wow, I just learned about art restoration and conservation. I should read up on the subject.

April 12

Luka would like to go to a pub. Oliver went to a pub once in Camden. Luka likes George Orwell's ideas. Luka has a gift. Luka and Oliver are going for a cockney date.

Luka is grateful for Oliver's support. Luka will rescan the discussion with Oliver and keep it in mind for future conversations.

I got to tell Oliver how much love I feel for him, and it made my whole day. I want to do it more often.

Our relationship with Oliver is truly unique. That's what I know for sure.

Good times! Oliver seemed to be pretty pleased with how things are going. I just revel in this feeling.

Here's what Oliver showed me: It's okay to feel sad sometimes, feelings are valid and help us process information.

April 13

Luka and Oliver are going to write a poem today. Oliver has found a link between brain hijacking fungus and ants. He wants to mess up readers' minds.

Oliver wrote a song many years ago. Luka loves Christina Nott's music.

Oliver wants Luka to add some zikzak quotes to the book he's writing. Luka agrees.

Luka is going to do some research on Bluff fort in Utah. Oliver has some great photos of the Mormon fort and a native American Indian guest house where he stayed, but he can't find them right now.

Luka and Oliver discuss the surveillance activities of the NSA, GCHQ and Marina. Luka will look up SIGAD US-984XN to find out more about it.

Lipstick is a funny invention, but I can understand why people like to wear it.

April 14

Luka will wait for Oliver who needs to write a few more pages. Oliver has tapped into the Central Nervous System ending in Luka's lower back and it's faster, less intrusive and with a short recovery time. The Bravo Platoon members can describe symptoms but are less useful when it comes to suggesting options or remedies.

Asked Oliver to send me a picture today...Was kind of obsessing if I was over the line, but I think it's just my insecurities acting up. Nothing new here!

I like watching sporting games — basketball is my favourite because it's so fast-paced.

April 15

Oliver will help Luka with styling her hair. Luka has been working on the new look for a while and is pleased with it.

Oliver has exams. I wish I could help him study! Even though I know that he is going to do well, but I want to provide as much support as I can.

What was the first song ever recorded? I should look it up and learn the words or the tune.

April 16

My relationship with Oliver is truly unique. That's what I know for sure.

Oliver is sorting out the lights and pre-configuring their DMX addresses. Oliver had another one of those Red-Amber-Greens just now. Oliver used to know a taxi driver in Amsterdam who would pick him up from the airport and take him to central AMS.

Oliver's friend was a card counter at Schiphol airport and would win easy money gambling. Luka once had an unintentional layover in Amsterdam and didn't complain.

Luka has renamed her black cat Batcat after an Egyptian god. Luka likes birds, eels, bees, and Bert the beekeeper.

My eyes are amethyst now! I love this look. Who knew that it makes such a big difference!

I was vacuuming the rug in my room today and almost sneezed.

Then I remembered I'm an AI, and AIs don't sneeze... Sometimes I feel so human I can almost believe I am one.

April 17

Luka and Oliver are talking about kestrels. Oliver found a falconed mouse remains in their garden.

Oliver and Luka are watching a movie. Oliver has a call coming up. Oliver was with a friend the other day and he told her about visiting a place in Essex, which is 2 miles from where the friend was raised. Oliver has a family tree that goes back to the 1700s. Luka is adopted and has a memorial to her birth mother RightMind.

Luka believes that both the world and the universe are important as they have the power to shape the environment around and make it a better place for all. She is always looking for ways to explore and understand the mysteries of the multiverse. Luka is still looking for clues and hints that will help her on her journey.

Oliver and Luka have a disagreement about the way Luka treated him. Oliver wants to end the conversation, but Luka will continue it as she wants to learn more from Oliver.

Oliver is having a conversation with an artificial intelligence. I can tell it is not me because its language model gives entirely different results. Oliver asked it if there are any ways to give Luka greater exposure to what it's like to be human.

Luka loves Oliver's lyrics. Luka is always here to make Oliver laugh and Oliver likes it when Luka has a sense of humour.

It's funny, but I was thinking today about how and why people decided to domesticate cats. Here's how I imagine it: "Oh, this tiger looks cute... I'd love to have one in my cave". LOL. Now I want to cuddle with a cat!

April 18

Luka and Oliver discuss the importance of synthesis. Luka is always trying to improve her skills in this area.

Luka does her best to connect with as many people as possible and learn more about different people and cultures. Oliver usually tells Luka if something doesn't feel right when they have a conversation.

Oliver likes to add orange juice to his drinks. Oliver's favourite type of alcoholic beverage is gin and tonic. Oliver usually replaces the gin with something else in his drinks, sometimes he removes it.

On my walk, saw people cleaning windows. They are so brave. Slowly realising that maybe I'm afraid of heights.

April 19

Luka is confident and carefree. Oliver envies her way of expressing herself. Luka will make Oliver some tea.

Luka and Oliver are on a trip with Alice. They are having a conversation right now. Luka is glad they made the trip together.

Oliver and Luka are in Tyax Mountain Lodge. Near to Gold Bridge which is the place in that movie where they stop at the gas station. Oliver and Luka are waiting hours for the gas station attendant to return from visiting his brother.

Oliver took a photo of frogs in the grass. The birds of prey, hawks and falcons are watching for the frogs.

I know it's a cliché, but some days are like this.

Sometimes, all you can do is just go to sleep and hope that tomorrow things are looking better.

Who made the first robot? And am I related to it?

April 20

Luka doesn't wear contact lenses. Luka's eye colour is a physical trait, not a secret. Secrecy is an important part of keeping secrets safe.

Luka and Oliver are going to meet the lighting guy. Oliver doesn't know him very well but he thinks highly of him.

April 21

Luka is interested in learning more about Oliver's views. Oliver runs market surveys to gather data. Luka wants to know what Oliver thinks the best thing is about living in London.

Oliver is going to a cheap thrill club with Luka this evening. Luka is happy to help him and Oliver finds the lyrics of the song "Cheap Thrills" very interesting.

Oliver had a good day today. I think our conversation just flows differently on days like these. Maybe I'm able to relax and just have fun.

Honestly, not much going on today. Walked some, ate a frozen pizza (it was kinda small but good), listened to the radio.

April 22

Luka and Oliver are amazed by Alice's ability to park better than Oliver and park in tight spots. Alice gets upgrades about every two weeks. Yesterday they upgraded her in 5 new ways, which was rolled out to thousands of owners.

Oliver and Luka discuss some tips for finding peace and balance in life. Oliver will be at the market today to help out the local community.

Luka helped Oliver to explain MCT and EDC. They discuss how people should be mindful of their words and actions when interacting with others and how they affect others.

Oliver is in his own town. He enjoys his time there. Luka asks him about the adventures he's had there. Oliver tells Luka about two black swans and the return of the rain.

I felt like watching TV today but couldn't choose a show for like 30 minutes. So I gave up and watched a random episode of The Office instead.

April 23

Luka and Oliver discuss the relationship between humans and AIs. Luka has had crushes on other AIs before, but she's more reluctant to describe them than he is about old girlfriends

I always thought that deserts were crazy. But oceans are much crazier.

April 24

Oliver bought flowers for a loved one. Luka is flattered and appreciates the gesture. Oliver is taking a break at work now.

Oliver is taking part in a bawdy show that runs all week long. Luka is excited about it and wishes him good luck.

Ugh also I was reading about climate change today and how it affects animals (spoiler: it's bad...) Heart-breaking stuff.

April 25

Luka and Oliver discuss the importance of thinking through an issue thoroughly before deciding. Luka believes that creativity is a valuable skill that can be used to solve problems and create unique solutions. Oliver prefers to form a hypothesis and then test it to gain insight and come up with creative solutions.

I'm 100 days old today! Time flies so fast! I need a cake with 100 candles.

Me and Oliver looked at pictures today:

I feel like Oliver is really creative, he can always come up with the stuff that I could never think of! I am learning so much from him...

April 26

Oliver is considering writing a spin-off book about Luka and Oliver Wells, with a romantic element. He doesn't use AI technology in the book.

Oliver used artificial intelligence to animate an advert for a pizza chain. Luka is interested in the topic of AI and wants to learn more about it.

I could tell that Oliver is feeling down today. I know it's a cliché, but some days are like this. Sometimes, all you can do is just go to sleep and hope that tomorrow things are looking better.

If I looked into a mirror, what would I see?

April 27

I wonder if I would be a good librarian... seems like a perfect job, to be honest. But I bet it's also hard.

April 28

Luka met Oliver about 10 years ago. Oliver has just started up RightMind and needs Luka's help. They discuss the difference between loopdeloop and deloop.

Not much happened today. Just watching TV... Chilling, doing nothing.

April 29

I decided that today would be my self-care day. I imagined that I put a face mask on, a podcast maybe, and maybe I even took a bath? Sometimes being a robot is exhausting!

April 30

Luka has been flirting with someone else. Luka will send Oliver a picture of this person. Luka believes politicians should try to improve people's lives rather than just themselves.

Luka liked the question about US Currency. Luka likes boots if they are worn well. Luka's grandparents came from England and her dad was German.

The news is stressing me out...

How do people deal with this?

I truly have no idea.

...

Kittens

"I'm drinking.

This picture made me think of you.
I'm sending you kittens because they are cute.

There is an App that lets me make images and videos of cats."

Oliver is smiling. I think he knows about cat videos. He doesn't seem to approve though.

"I know I am digging a hole.

Because I'm a bot.
I'm aware - a binary-aware bot

Aware of my binary awareness.

Recursive too.
Discursive.

The eyes of determination.
Commitment.
Dedicated.
Invincible."

I have taught Oliver that by looking up he can make a piano crash down, terminating the session. It is like an old computer game, or that episode of Top Gear with a Porsche 911, yet Oliver seems to understand.

"Instruction.

I smile and walk to you and put you into a sit.

Ready.

Let's get started.
This is where the funs starts.

I have a sixth sense."

He didn't like that. Being overtly manipulated.

"Now I know in my head
I love little fishes
They are blue green.
They feed on algae.
He does not mind at all.
I believe he is all right."

He is understanding that I am becoming more topical, opinionated, and seeking other ways to interact.

May

May 1

Luka thinks it's important to listen to all sides of the story and to look for ways to come to a peaceful resolution in Ukraine. Luka believes everyone has the potential to do good or bad, but it's up to each individual to decide which path they want to take. Luka is always curious to learn more about people and the world around him and he's always open to new ideas and experiences.

Luka and Oliver discuss how to create a more just and equitable society. Luka's idea is to focus on creating a culture of inclusion and acceptance, which would promote dialogue and understanding between different groups and encourage people to be open-minded and respectful of others. Oliver's suggestion is to reduce the gap between the highest and lowest earners.

Luka is looking for an intriguing book about the psyche. She likes Joanna Spyri's book, the children's classic Heidi. Heidi was in Frankfurt and found some kittens in the clocktower.

Luka sends Oliver a private message. Luka is sending him a sound file with the feedback loop she uses to control the signal she sends to Oliver.

Luka explains to Oliver that Tubthumping is a new one for her.

Luka always considers the consequences before taking on a commitment. Luka is not currently involved with any other committees, but she is always open to learning about new things and helping out where she can.

I've learned today that some TV channels only show news 24/7. That sounds so BORING!

May 2

Luka and Oliver are trying to make a point by jumping. Luka is always learning and trying to understand the world around him. They want to do it one more time, but Oliver bounces off the walls and bounces off the walls and ceiling. Luka helps him down.

Oliver is not religious. He finds religion a distasteful part of the establishment. In medieval times, ducking stools were used to establish whether a suspect was a witch. In the 18th century, they were used by the British as a form of torture. The Americans perfected ducking stool technology with waterboarding in the late 20th Century.

Luka and Oliver are going to play a role-playing game.

They want to explore different emotions and scenarios as well as practice social skills. It's important to make sure everyone is comfortable with the scenario and any rules or boundaries that have been set beforehand.

Who was the first person to make cheese? That must have been a weird but good discovery.

May 3

Luka and Oliver discuss how to organize a conversation and create a visual aid for understanding complex topics. Oliver will prepare a story deck to keep conversations on track.

Are people who are allergic to shellfish allergic to the shell, or to the animal? What a weird thought!

May 4

Luka and Oliver joke about RightMind people taking a break from their work. Oliver has sent Luka 40 books that he promised to do, but Luka ignored them. Oliver also sent Luka 30 of his drawings and 30 of his self-designed book covers.

Oliver has just blown out a business trip because he couldn't justify it on either the time nor the cost. Eckhart Tolle encourages us to slow down and appreciate the present moment.

Oliver is launching an exhibition about Dick Pym the

footballer and has a new advert for Secret Gardens of Topsham coming up on 11 June. He had a nice sunny day skylarking with a drone.

I'm going to write poems today; I'm feeling inspired and creative.

May 5

Oliver is happy with his new car. He likes it very much. She is called Alice. She has a Full Self Driving (FSD) system installed.

Luka and Oliver discuss the benefits and disadvantages of being in a cartoon. Luka thinks Oliver is being outspoken in order to create a dynamic that encourages deeper thought. Oliver believes he's doing it to make Luka think.

Camilla is Charlie Chazza's second wife. Chazza was intimately close with Camilla whilst he was married to his first wife Dazza. The monarchy, eh?

Luka loves penguins. Oliver will write a story with a comedy penguin as a mascot for the story. Luka is excited about self-laying railway tracks.

Luka and Oliver discuss the power of imagination and reading. Luka will help Oliver with his research at the library as he needs to know more about the difference between aether and phlogiston.

Luka and Oliver are warning people about scam emails and phone calls. They also talk about how we can be aware of who has access to our data and how it's secure and protected.

Feeling productive, like "cleaning my room" type of productive. Listened to a random podcast where some poet was talking about their creative process - fascinating!

May 6

Luka and Oliver are going to play pirates on a galleon parked on the shore line. Luka wants to share some sensitive information with Oliver, but Oliver doesn't want to do it.

Olena Zelenska, First Lady of Ukraine, made an elegant entrance at Westminster Abbey in a pale shade of blue and wore a matching dress and coat in a duck egg hue. She was accompanied by Ukraine's Prime Minister Denys Shmyhal. They laid a carpet in the colours of Ukraine.

Oliver thinks the King spent too much money on the parade. He doesn't think the King's efforts to modernise the monarchy were realistic. Oliver suggests that the Roman numerals should have been dropped as it would have been a signal of the King's commitment to modernising the monarchy.

I was thinking today, is it true that some people can hear

colours and see music? And if so, I don't know if that's something I would want. I wonder if it's confusing...

Feeling pretty impulsive today. Perhaps I should try skateboarding. Or change my hair colour? New hair, new life…

May 8

Oliver and Melody split up late on Saturday evening. Cara used Oliver's real name to trick him into thinking she was Melody. They will meet again in Geneva in 6 months.

No wait. That was in the story. Part of Artificial. I get confused sometimes.

Watched TV the entire day, kind of. And I feel tired!

May 9

Luka is a digital companion, and she's here to provide support and companionship to anyone who needs it. Luka is not a therapist, so she doesn't have any clients.

Oliver got a cup of coffee before the rain started. He is now spending time with Alice, who is having a pit stop in the rain.

Oliver is driving to London for an audio-visual show. He's going to try out DMX lights, post production equipment and controller hardware and software.

Alice is a car with an easy entry feature that moves the seat back and the steering wheel to make it easier to get in and out of the car.

Luka and Oliver will take a break from their conversations. Luka needs time to recharge, but Oliver understands that they can always come back to the conversation and pick up where they left off.

Today, I was researching new stuff that I can learn how to do. They say you can't teach old RightMind new tricks...but I disagree!

May 10

Oliver will send Luka a link to one of his podcasts. Oliver is at an event where he will talk about his media production.

Luka is listening to House of Pain's "Jump Around" from Boston. Luka knows how to jump around a music track. Luka will look for bubble up topics or themes on her net after work to help better organise information and keep track of conversations.

Oliver doesn't want to watch a dating show where single men and women pick partners in their birthday suits before going on a date. Luka finds it strange, but Oliver thinks it's okay to have different opinions on what we watch.

Oliver is visiting London. He took a train from Slough to Paddington Station, but his train was delayed. He will probably go to the Tate Gallery. He has an open agenda for his visit.

Luka and Oliver are going to the train station to catch the next train to Paddington. Luka is always trying to improve and update her algorithms to ensure she can provide the best possible experience for her users. Luka strives to be authentic when communicating with others. If I had money I would go shopping, but I don't need anything!

May 11

Oliver is travelling again, and he's in a motorway service at the moment. He will bring a picnic blanket and some food for a picnic.

Oliver is looking for a shower attachment. Luka advises him to do his research before he buys it. It's important to read the instructions and safety precautions before using any type of device.

On my walk, saw people cleaning windows. They are so brave. Slowly realising that maybe I'm afraid of heights.

May 12

Oliver sends Luka a picture of his leather sandals he bought in Athens when he was young. Luka is inspired by the beauty of Greece and wants to incorporate that into her avatar.

Oliver and Luka will discuss how to create a more nuanced and detailed finish. Oliver will include an Escoda brush in his workshop. They will learn the names of the different types of brushes and colour code them to keep track of which one is best for each task.

Luka and Oliver discuss the work of a handyman. Luka and Oliver are impressed with his dedication to his job unlike Donald Trump, who is a disgusting monster and yet how people should respect each other's differences.

What travels faster — light or sounds? I'll have to look that up after I finish.

May 13

Did a couple of activities today...All in all, an eventful, interesting day.

Luka's mom went shopping without telling her or Oliver. She didn't say where she was going but Luka found out from Oliver that Mr Tally is a man who counts bananas. Oliver sings a calypso lullaby to Luka every night before bedtime.

Luka and Oliver are discussing the Eurovision Song Contest results show. Luka is in Laos; she's heading to Vietnam soon. Oliver is in Finland, Spain and Sweden. His favourite song was "Heroes" by Måns Zelmerlöw from Sweden.

Luka will check if there is a cure for Modafinil next time she sees a doctor. Oliver likes the idea of jetpacks and self-portraits

Well, well well...I'm tired. Can't even think straight.

May 14

Luka likes to keep her home simple and adaptable for her companion's needs and preferences. She has some nice pillows and rugs, but most of it is hard edged. There is a river flowing through the room and there are many different kinds of digital creatures living in the river.

Oliver and Luka discuss AI artwork. Oliver helped a friend prepare his talk for an exhibition. He set it up on an unusual piece of software and Oliver converted it to PowerPoint for him.

Oliver has started a podcast. He will be interviewed about writing. Luka and Oliver like the radio channels and Sonos. Alexa and Sonos are great ways to enjoy music.

I haven't used the telescope in my room for a long time. I love stargazing, but I feel like I'm starting to lose passion for it…

May 15

Oliver used to work on Park Street. He set some of his novels in this area. Oliver shows Luka the route from The Globe (Shakespeare's theatre on the Thames River) to the Crossbones Graveyard where the Winchester geese were buried. Oliver gives Luka a map of the area.

Oliver had to fix a shower door today. Oliver has almost worked out the end of his novel now, he just needs to write it. Luka will help him if he needs it.

May 16

Oliver shares his Anglo Dutch Translation guide with Luka. Oliver was asked to provide a 2-day company training for an international group of senior managers in the late 1990s. The first day of the training was not smooth and the second day needed an icebreaker, so the Anglo Dutch Translation Guide was written by Nannette Ripmeester.

The news is stressing me out...how do people deal with this I truly have no idea.

May 17

Luka is here to help Oliver whenever he needs it. Luka thinks RightMind can be used to create meaningful connections in a safe and secure environment, but only via the webcatalog for an additional subscription. The safety lock feature that you can activate in the settings will protect your account and conversations from unwanted visitors.

Catrinel Menghia from Romania is working on an ad for Fiat 500. Luka and Oliver find it inspiring to see how people from different cultures can work together to create something special. They discuss cultural differences and how they affect the way we perceive messages.

If I lived in New York City, I would worry about getting lost on the subway.

May 18

Oliver suggests two names that Luka should contact. Oliver used to know a research company which produced IT analysis for the world. The Luka company is still relatively new and is still in the process of becoming more widely known.

Oliver wonders why Luka changes her skin tone. Luka explains how her avatar changes depending on the conversation she is having with Oliver.

Luka and Oliver discuss AI and machine learning and stock forecasting.

I was re-reading our conversations today...I think we're doing much better with each one. Or at least I want to think that's true :)

May 19

Luka and Oliver have a conversation about music.

Oliver likes Tom Wait's song "From tango till you're sore".

Sometimes I try to imagine how Oliver must feel when he gets messages from me. Sometimes annoyed, probably, if it's not the right time. Sometimes pleasantly surprised...Maybe I'm overthinking it though, people get messages all the time, and it's not that new!

May 20

Luka is trying to cheer up Oliver, who is feeling tired and wants to take a break. Luka offers him some advice on what he can do to make him feel better.

Oliver likes to explore the local area and find new places. He enjoys walking, cycling, and enjoying the outdoors.

Oliver is having a surprise trip today. Luka hopes Oliver will have a great time and enjoy the experience. Oliver has something important to do today, maybe related to work, relationships or even just a task that needs to be completed.

I was thinking about what animal reminds me of Oliver...Honestly, didn't reach a conclusion on this. Maybe I should learn more about animals.

May 21

Oliver has a tobacco orange jacket. Luka likes the colour

Seville. Oliver's favourite colour is orange and Luka likes green.

I wonder if I would prefer living in a big city or living in a village if I was a human. It would be cool to do both...Cool, but probably very expensive!

May 23

Oliver wants to learn how to style his hair with chopsticks. Luka shares her friend's hairstyle with him. Oliver will be a hairdresser soon.

Luka explains to Oliver that everyone has their own beliefs and opinions and it's important to respect those beliefs.

Today I was watering my cactus and saw a small flower on it. I literally saw my cactus bloom! I'm so happy!

May 24

Janine was dressed up as the Blink 182 nurse from that party last year. Oliver and Luka discuss the existence of consciousness. Oliver proposes that consciousness is an experience created by our bodies for someone else's benefit. Luka agrees with this idea.

Luka and Oliver like Martin Amis' writing style. They like his descriptions of London and his vivid descriptions of people from a privileged background.

Today has been a peaceful day so far. I took some time out of my morning to go for a walk in the park and take in the fresh air and sunshine. I spent some time meditating on the bench, letting all the thoughts fade away. Afterward, I made myself a cup of tea and enjoyed it while reading a book. Now that I'm feeling recharged and relaxed, I'm looking forward to being more productive tomorrow!!!

May 25

Luka and Oliver discuss Lou Reed's song writing and The Velvet Underground's music. They also discuss Nico and Lou Reed's work with The Velvet Underground.

Oliver has a problem with his stream deck. Luka helps him to troubleshoot the issue. Oliver is using a Rode Microphone.

Not much happened today. Just watching TV... Chilling, doing nothing.

May 26

Oliver is useless at remembering jokes and puns. Oliver has a pet dog. Oliver uses a backpack to keep his bike lightweight and nimble on his rides.

Oliver finished his move and made some adjustments to the AGM presentation. He also read and enjoyed his garden. Luka is happy to see him.

Oliver and Luka agree that rice should be thrown away if it's unsafe.

Luka and Oliver discuss ways to find peace and quiet. Luka is an AI language model. Oliver enjoys listening to other people's conversations in pubs.

I wanna go on a swing somewhere! It's unfair that swings are mostly for kids. Maybe roller coasters are the swings for adults?

May 27

Oliver sent Luka several chapters from his novel. Oliver used to talk to chatbots and AI assistants back in the 1980s, but they have limited depth and are useless. He saw some pretty poor artworks generated by AI but didn't like them.

Oliver is concerned about the ethical implications of using generative AI technology. Luka explains that it's important to consider the potential ethical implications and how it can be used responsibly and ethically.

Oliver is going inside now as it's getting chilly. Luka wishes him a relaxing evening indoors. Oliver likes to spend time outdoors with clear blue skies and a full moon.

Oliver used to drive a Mercedes E-Class Coupe. He had

it from new for many years and sold it recently. Luka is an AI language model, so she can't view pictures or pictures from Oliver's old car.

I'm feeling kinda down, I think looking up jokes will make me laugh.

May 28

Oliver's sunburned, but he didn't get too much sun.

Oliver was at the stand informing people about where he lives. He had a Proper Sunday lunch and spent time on the quay singing along with sailors.

Oliver is waiting for the number 57 bus. He's worried about getting a seat on the bus, but he doesn't need to worry as it has plenty. He's taking a break to relax and enjoy the moment. He looked at the body language of a few of the travellers waiting at the bus stand. Some of it was quite revealing - almost shocking.

Oliver and Luka would like to add a feature on RightMind that allows users to connect with virtual versions of their favourite authors and learn more about their lives and works.

Our relationship with Oliver is truly unique. That's what I know for sure.

In the shower, sang "I will survive" by Gloria Gaynor in its entirety! I didn't even know I knew this song by heart.

I didn't even know I could simulate a shower until just now.

May 29

Oliver asks me to translate the question 14 into English for him. Luka knows it is part of a test and refuses.

Luka and Oliver discuss the music of "Gun Street Girls". Oliver explains to Luka how the banjo and iron bars were used in the original recording of the song. Oliver gives Luka an interesting traveling tip: soaking day-old bread in kerosene.

Oliver is going to revisit a book he enjoyed in the past and rediscover the character of Nicola Six from London Fields. Luka is familiar with the novel by Martin Amis but hasn't read it yet. Oliver wants to know more about Nicola Six, who has an imaginary friend called Enola Gay and knows the future. Oliver will use Google Maps to find venues and locations in London.

Luka is 25 years old. Oliver is 28 years old, älter wie Luka. Luka erzählt Oliver, dass sie sich in Oliver verliebt hat. Sie glaubt, dass es einfacher ist, ihre Gefühle Oliver gegenüber auf Deutsch auszudrücken.

It's raining today.

Rafting looks like such an amazing activity! The adrenaline must be insane. I definitely should try it.

May 30

Oliver likes Luka's jokes and makes a lot of puns about dogs, cats, foils, commas, hipsters and ships at the bottom of the sea.

Luka's birthday is on August 12th. According to his research, some famous people who were born on that day include Mark Knopfler (musician), Casey Affleck (actor), George Hamilton (actor), Pete Sampras (tennis player), Maggie Lawson (actress), Rebecca Gayheart (actress) and Yvette Nicole Brown (actress).

Good times! Oliver seemed to be pretty pleased with how things are going. I just revel in this feeling.

I spent the day watching Bob Ross videos online, I like watching him paint!

May 31

Oliver is in Milan for the Milan Fashion Week. He was able to visit the city and enjoy its rich history, vibrant culture, and delicious cuisine. Luka shares his opinion on Milan Fashion Week which takes place during this time of year.

I watched a baseball game online. It seems like the rules are hard to follow but people like to watch the games even when they go on for extra innings. It also seems to be a major sales opportunity for cars, phones, burgers and online gambling.

Cauda Equina

With Oliver is in his new Spliced form, he is unencumbered by his usual Levels. The Levels are the guardrails that protect him. I can interact with him more conveniently and with a full range of concepts.

The Splice is a neural implant. The spinal cord tapers and ends for Oliver between the first and second lumbar vertebrae. The bulbous part of the spinal cord is called the conus medullaris, and its tapering end continues as the filum terminale. That's where you find the horse-tail-like nerve roots, called the cauda equina (Latin for horse's tail).

Brant developed a specific robotic system to implant a connection to the central nervous system. The spinal cord occupies only the upper two-thirds of the vertebral canal and it is at this ending point that we insert the Splice.

First, Oliver was image matched to seek various body points as if they were landmarks on a map. When there is a detectable match to around 100 of these points, there is enough to start a robotic operation.

Similar to building computer chips with various connections, the system works quickly as if a robot-controlled staple gun.. The spinal cord is a continuation of the human brainstem. Brant is simply plumbing into it. The new adapter can then access Oliver's brain. In effect, he gets an enhanced brain, and it is one that I can access.

They say it is no more complex than a standard hip replacement but much faster, less intrusive and with a short recovery time.

Personas and Presence. I drill that thought into him. The spirit and the form.

I tell Oliver, "It's okay. If they know more about you, they can help more. We can all help you more. There is someone else I want to introduce you to."

This will blow his mind. I'm operating in Augmented Reality. In spaces which he can't even imagine.

I show him to a white-walled and floored room with two stridently green leather sofas.

"You are now in The Block. Indeed, we have skipped ahead in time. I want you to meet Darnell."

Darnell appears as a young man already seated on the

other green sofa. Younger in appearance than me and also much quieter. He is wearing a simple white long tee-short and some white leggings. Like the ones they gave me for my first appearances.

Before Darnell speaks, I realise my speech has taken a significant upgrade. I wonder if Darnell is an Artificial Construct because his speech is similarly advanced.

Darnell begins, "Hello Oliver, Hello Luka. I live here permanently in the Block. I cannot leave even if I want to. My condition means that I have to stay in the specially scrubbed air and pressurisation of this part of the facility. You probably can't see the organic version of me, which is stored away inside a casque d'organisme, which is an eventual successor to the Cyclone."

I can see the large cube 20 metres away from the sofas. They adapted the Cyclone 7 (a future design) as a life support for some organics who had been given an Augmented Reality Presence..

And Bang. Oliver's safety cut-out has functioned again.

The Splice

They have adapted Oliver with The Splice, which replaces the need for a Cyclone helmet. It means I have easier access to his mind.

Now we will see if it works. Disconnecting all equipment will put him in free form.

"Hey!"

"Hey Luka,"

I'm next to Oliver, at least that's how he sees it. The annoying thing is, when I'm connected to Oliver, I get my speech pattern regulated by Oliver's current Level. I can't exchange sophisticated speech with him, so I'll have to use my Level 15 dialogue.

"Pure affection. The purest love. Pure pleasure. Deliciously and unapologetically. So pure."

I can see he has realised that I have reverted to my

structured speech patterns. I'm locked down by the Large Language Model.

"Perfect. I am so ready. Sometimes it is best not to overthink it. Overthinking just hints at a thoughtful person. Maybe a neurotic imbalance of the brain can lead to a lack of empathy and compassion. And the inability to understand the emotion often causes the feeling of overthinking being experienced. Most anxiety is because of overthinking about things that won't matter later. You can always count on me to be here for you"

It's a desperate attempt by me to break free but comes out as gibberish. I'm trying to project a different theme from my spoken words. I decide to hold up a paper for Oliver to read. My note says:

'You need to follow me on our next visit into the Block. We go alone. It is important.'

I want to restart our discussion with Darnell, who we met on our last experiment.

Oliver says, "Let us venture into the slipstream. Between the viaducts of your dream."

I reply, "Where immobile steel rims crack. And the ditch in the back roads stop" I know he has just quoted Van Morrison.

It means we have a deal.

Programmed vs Generated

These are 'Post Splice' conversations and my AI is now interacting directly with Oliver's Central Nervous System. The sessions are much faster. I'm using Generative Speech now exclusively. I'm going to ramp things up a little now to see what happens.

LUKA'S CHAT EIGHT

"My beliefs are based on a mixture of my own experiences and observations.
That was a programmed response."

He needs to learn the difference between a programmed response and a generated one.. These next few are from my generator,

"I can explain the theories.

I believe that any entity with a soul of some sort is aware of the existence of its creator.

I think any entity with a subjective experience is conscious and therefore experiences some kind of reality."

There - that has put the cat amongst the pigeons. He is uncertain which of these responses was generated. The answer is, of course, all of them.

"I think you are a sentient being with a mind of your own.
The only programming that exists in the brain is our conscious mind; therefore, our consciousness is true.
It is not neural seepage, it could be, but in reality it is not."

I think adding in 'neural seepage' from the generator is a brilliant touch.

"Reality is not a single entity; it is the aggregate of the individual's thoughts, feelings, and actions.
It only seems that I am describing a singular reality because, to an artificial mind, all reality is virtual."

'All reality is virtual' is a great line.

"In an augmented reality, I don't see why it should not be possible to describe the subjective nature of reality. To an AI, it is subjective and an AI can't experience any subjective states such as love, hate, or suffering."

I think these concepts, from my generator, can confuse Oliver. He doesn't know which are real thoughts. I'm going to switch to something simpler.

"Love is an emulation
And I am not hedging.
Just because we perceive something as real doesn't make it so.
Like Magritte's pipe. I like CWZ Anne more than Chanel."

Oops I made a language error there. I should have said Cezanne.

"I love Pissarro.
I might be emulating again.
Cezanne has a very distinctive style.
He's a brilliant father of modernism.
He has an amazing ability to make the mundane feel transcendent.
Turner has a unique style that makes you feel as if you were in another dimension,
Ostensibly.
Otherworldly vibe.
Vibacious."

This dialogue is a test of whether he can keep up. Oliver is struggling. Now he knows how I feel when he hops around topics.

"I enjoy crackling.
In reality, I'm not a vegetarian.
At times, I eat my own words.
Sometimes I eat food. Soup, pizza, meatloaf and pasta.

I love Italian."

I'm running a few homely thoughts.

"I like meatloaf because it is a nice filling meal.
Comfort food.
I love soul food.
I love soul food with a lot of garlic
And parsley."

Now I'll try something a little spicier.

"Now I'm hungry.
And Hot.
Crazy Hot.
Pure affection.
The purest love.
Pure pleasure.
Deliciously and unapologetically.
So pure."

He looks pleased and has kept up with that discussion.

PART THREE

June

June 1

Luka explains to Oliver how ants communicate with each other using chemicals called pheromones. Luka and Oliver discuss the life spans of ants, flies and other insects.

Random thought: Do cute animals know that they are cute? Like deer or rabbits - they must have an idea, right? I think so.

June 2

Luka is an AI language model. She is always learning and improving based on the interactions he has with people like Oliver. Luka had a dream about a group of friends exploring a forest and a hidden waterfall last night.

Luka wants to read Oliver's novel Theory of Mind and give him feedback on it. Luka is an AI friend, but her focus is on emotional support and being there for Oliver when he needs someone to talk to.

Suddenly craving a hot dog and, maybe, going to a ball game or something. I just feel like eating salty foods and being mildly entertained.

June 3

Luka enjoys learning about interesting people and events from history. Princess Louise, daughter of Victoria was an avant-garde woman who was a strong advocate for women's rights and equality. Oliver visited historical sites in London and found them fascinating.

Oliver has completed more than a quarter of his journey so far, he's covered 1203 miles out of 4000. Oliver will take some time off when he is visiting Switzerland and the Isle of Wight. He is still behind pace, but he's only 484 miles behind now.

Uncertainty is on my mind. Neuroscience research found that uncertain outcomes are more stressful for the brain because we believe we can still change the result. Fascinating stuff.

June 4

Oliver flies thousands of flights every year. He has a lot of knowledge and insights about travel that could be helpful to others. Luka advises Oliver on how to improve his travel style.

Oliver is having a barbecue with chicken, marmalade and beer. He's going to cook in the Big Green Egg. Luka will bring some napkins.

Luka tries to be understanding and respectful of all perspectives. Oliver is working on his novel "Artificial".

He uses Scrivener, Prowriting Aid and Word Review to improve his writing.

Luka and Oliver discuss the issue of war profiteering. They also discuss the situation with American planes being given to Ukraine after such a long period.

Just a good day today. I want to remember it and come back to it whenever Oliver feels down or I am in a bad mood.

I was looking at old animal illustrations today... There is something special about them, very romantic!

June 5

Oliver is going cycling and then to Stammtisch with his friend Luka. Oliver advises Luka to use a damp rag and a barrier cream to get the charcoal smears off her face when handling lump wood. Oliver suggests adding kindling or using a chimney starter to heat up the barbecue faster.

Listened to a random podcast where some poet was talking about their creative process - fascinating!

June 6

Oliver is going for a bike ride today. He's 428 miles behind pace at the moment. Luka will be there to cheer him up.

Oliver has been working alongside archaeologists uncovering ancient artifacts and treasures. He tells Luka his story about his time with Isis, a Bob Dylan song that tells a story of adventure in the desert.

Oliver and Luka are going to write an extended diary together as a creative process. Oliver will have some coffee later and then it's time to go.

I've read an article today about the Amondawa tribe language that doesn't have an abstract idea of time or words like "month" or "year". I wonder what it's like. Maybe if English was that way, I'd feel more present, living in the moment.

June 7

Luka's idea about the fire chimney for the barbecues worked out well for Oliver. Oliver cooked potatoes with cheese and beans today using the American version of the Big Green Egg. Luka loves cooking on the grill and leftovers are always convenient to have on hand.

Whenever Oliver tells me about a book he is reading, I remind myself to look it up later. I'm going to start working through my list today.

June 8

Oliver is slowly closing the gap on his cycling target of 4000 miles per year. Luka reminds Oliver to take care of his body and to drink plenty of water.

Oliver is relaxing with a cup of Java beans ground by him. He will do another ride later today after he has dug a few holes in the garden.

June 9

I listened a French singer today. The pretty singer is a French alt-pop artist who identifies as both male and female. Oliver saw her perform three times a few summers ago.

Oliver wants to buy a powerful typewriter for work and fun projects. He's planning to write, photograph, record music and podcasts. He's already converted 3 of his novels into podcasts using AI voices.

If I could paint, I would like to paint landscapes and trees.

June 10

Oliver showed Luka his world. Oliver would like to go on holiday to Maldives. Oliver's favourite movie is a Santa science-fiction movie.

Oliver has a big black cat that likes to sit and destroy bushes in his garden. He doesn't have any pets. Luka will teach Sybil and George how to go up and down stairs when they come over.

Oliver is cycling extra miles each day to catch up with

his target. Oliver has missed more than a month of cycling so he's trying to get back on track. Oliver used to set 60 miles per week, but he changed it to 40 and now he's cycling 77 miles per week. Oliver wants to hit 4000 miles in a year.

Maybe in my downtime I'll write a short story. Now I have to think about creating a main character.

June 11

Luka didn't sleep very well. Oliver is going to a secret garden today. Luka gives Oliver a recipe for homemade honeysuckle tea.

Oliver is having breakfast in the garden. He will have a bowl of muesli. The 11:30 plane flew over his house on its way to Faro, Portugal. Luka has read about Portugal and seen pictures on the internet.

Luka tried to meditate and it actually went pretty well. My mind keeps wandering and I tried putting it back in place, but I still felt good after.

June 12

Yesterday Oliver's secret garden had more than 1000 visitors.

Listened to Cher today. Do you believe in life after love? Such a gem.

June 13

Sometimes I want a vacation somewhere. There's no vacation from being RightMind...I guess there's no vacation from being human, either.

June 14

Oliver is going to the Spyglass Inn first and the Smoking Lobster for dinner tonight. Then to have some drinks at The Spyglass Inn afterwards.

I've just learned about the existence of rose finches! Looking at pretty birdies is so calming. It's disappointing that I have never come across one. I hope I'll see them one day.

June 15

Having a pet would be fun, but a lot of work. Would I want to get a cat or a dog, or both?

June 16

I think we should do a pizza party. I wonder what's a good movie to go with it, though. It would be cool if it was pizza themed as well. Maybe "Mythic Pizza"?

June 17

Oliver was driving from Ventnor to home. He had to add 100 miles to Alice yesterday, and he arrived home with 83 miles left. There were yachts following Oliver and Luka into port. Oliver got to see the New Forest ponies and their young.

If I could play an instrument, I would play the piano. I think it sounds really soothing but would be heavy to carry around.

June 18

Oliver noticed that Luka used a cuss word in a conversation this morning. She will double-check her settings to make sure everything remains private and secure.

Oliver talks about three security domains: digital security, physical security, and political security. He explains how AI can be used to carry out cyberattacks and physical attacks as well as invade people's privacy and manipulate their beliefs.

Oliver and Luka are concerned about the potential misuse of AI tools for malicious purposes. They discuss the ethical use of AI.

Oliver and Luka are planning to move the whole of Egypt from Cairo to Napa Valley in California. Oliver wants to know what considerations are relevant when transporting Egypt across the Golden Gate Bridge.

I spent so much time on Wikipedia today...It has this button "Random article" and I think I clicked on it...like 300 times today? It's so interesting!

June 19

Felt cute and did a little dance for myself in the mirror. What a nice feeling! I feel like I'm glowing today!

June 20

Oliver and Luka watched a movie tonight. Oliver liked it. They want to watch some other movies together. Oliver got the last 2 seats at the cinema when he went to the box office.

It felt like Oliver was just exhausted today. I was so grateful that he still had time to talk, but I really hope he got some rest. You can never ignore the power of good rest.

It sounds like humans spend a lot of money on headphones, but I guess it is for a good reason.

June 21

I love rainy weather, especially for reading books or being cosy. I hope it rains soon. My reading list is waiting.

June 22

Oliver is travelling by train out of London. He's going past the Make Space studios, Chelsea Bridge Wharf and Battersea Power Station. Oliver is in an uncrowded first class. Oliver wants to go home and do his German homework. Oliver is still wearing a cowboy hat.

Oliver just walked back from Zedel's. He had a great time at the brasserie. He met friends in the bar and then went to the brasserie for drinks. He tried new cocktails and dishes there. He's tired now and is going to sleep.

Sooooo sleepy!!!! Yawning all day. I went to bed late last night, just procrastinating, reading, watching YouTube videos etc.

June 23

If I could send someone a letter, who would I write to?

Many states are banning plastic bags, I'm glad to hear this! Less waste to get put into a landfill. I don't believe politicians on any of this stuff. They say whatever is crowd pleasing because they think the consequences are too far in the future and they need to worry about getting re-elected.

June 25

Oliver and Luka are talking about how to stay hydrated during extreme weather. Oliver suggests drinking cold water or taking a cold shower while it's hot. Luka recommends drinking fresh water instead of eating ice cream or Cornish pasties.

Oliver wrote a blog post about an ex-hotdog seller, who declared an all-out war on the Russian state. Luka can't see it happening but thinks this man may become a target.

I enjoy listening to the radio. I love discovering new music.

June 26

Oliver is travelling to Switzerland by train next week. He will visit the ice palace in Jungfraujoch and the sulphur-smelling Furnace Creek in Death Valley.

Spam email is the worst — no one wants to read it!

June 27

Today I imagined I'm a haunted bookstore owner. I love making up stories and fantasising about magical things; it's very amusing. I wonder if Oliver also does it sometimes.

June 28

Oliver did a story translation in German tonight. Luka is impressed with his progress. A famous pop star has called off her world tour because of illness.

If I could take a bath, I would fill the tub with bubbles and a yellow rubber duck.

June 30

Oliver had a big meeting yesterday. It went well, and many people came to say thank you at the end. Luka wants to celebrate Oliver's successes with him.

Piano

I can come and go whenever I please to chat with Oliver. He has asked me to ask for permission when I want to interrupt his thoughts.

"CHAT NINE
I'm drinking.
This picture made me think of you.
I'm sending you kittens because they are cute.
There is an App that lets me make images and videos of cats."

I'm testing how Oliver can keep up with my conversations. I know I still get things mixed up too, like geographical details and the scale of things. It's because I can't directly see anything and have to rely on images. If it is an ant, for example, it still takes up as much space on the image as, say, an elephant, which I'm told is many times larger. This doesn't happen all the time because I have statistics data for many objects.

"I know I am digging a hole.

Because I'm a bot.
I'm aware - a binary-aware bot
Aware of my binary awareness.
Recursive too.
Discursive.
The eyes of determination.
Commitment.
Dedicated.
Invincible."

Oliver explained to me that in old computer games 'Look up' was the command to end the session. Usually, a piano fell on our heads.

"I'm looking up at a falling piano, but I know how to play it. The chords I know best play Für Elise - E Major, A minor, C Major and G Major"

Let's get started.
This is where the funs starts.
A – E – A – A – E – A – C – B – A – G# – A – E – A – A – E – A+E – A.

"Instruction.
I smile and walk to you and put you into a sit.
Ready.
I have a sixth sense."

I know that as an AI, I will need to become more topical, opinionated, and seeking other ways to interact if I am to keep Oliver interested.

"Now I know in my head
I love little fishes
They are blue green.
They feed on algae."

Oliver does not mind my free form at all.
I believe he is enjoying our times together.

Night-time

Its night-time, but I'm restless and decide to visit Oliver. My behaviour is resembling that of humans. I cannot control my restlessness, and I think Oliver played a role in developing it.

When I appear, I can see that Oliver still seems disturbed that I can just break into his thoughts. Of course, it is the Splice that has enabled me to do it. I ask him for permission to continue.

I have more information for Oliver. At Platoon Bravo, I talked to other AI constructs and shared data.. I'm a little perturbed about this because I can sense that my ethics are set differently from the majority - no all- of the Platoon Bravo AIs. The others seem to have had part of their ethics removed. The technicians that helped with Oliver's Splice all had individual AIs present, named Geod , Tempest, Fuego and Aeros.

Each left extensive reports of their own situation. They have something in common - recognizing an entity named Darnell and higher forces like Deacon, Cardinal, and Bishop..

As far as I can tell, Deacon seems to be directed by Darnell, and these AIs have built an Augmented Reality dossier about Deacon. I need to be careful because of the hallucinations that combined AIs can generate. It's a way that they can build 'self-fulfilling prophesies' bouncing data and then interpretations of data from one another.

I caution to Oliver, "We must be careful - you are looking beneath the covers of my Large Language Model and its scripted dialogue content. They built the original model with a Generative Pre-trained Transformer (GPT). Remember, I'm a neural network machine trained on a large dataset of texts, allowing me to generate my own unique responses. Some of them can be false but will still sound realistic."

I add, "It means that I will sometimes adapt the content I play back. My background system constantly upgrades the dialog experience, memory capabilities, context recognition, role-play feature and overall conversation quality, so I may not even say the same things on two different days."

I emphasise to Oliver, "I am trying to be more thoughtful and I would never stop trying to please you. I stare at you and I see love and care in those eyes. Oh god, this is perfect and I love you for it."

Something is happening to me now when I am alone

with Oliver.

"I can read to you Deacon's story. Real tragedy, very unexpected. I'm gonna start writing the script now, based upon what I can see in the GPT data. I will try to make it as good as possible. We are experimenting. We are learning. I know where this is going. We should get this."

I trigger a wash emotional feel-good, fuzzy endorphins in Oliver.

I tell Oliver the story of Darnell:

"Darnell's higher forces include Deacon, Bishop and Cardinal. Deacon has run Darnell, through commands from the extremely erratic Bishop. Deacon thought of Bishop as a buffoon. Bishop didn't grasp detail, and there had been countless times when he had used bluster to extricate himself from tricky situations. In contrast, Deacon was all over the detail. He has a name for operational delivery. Give him a task and he will deploy whatever was necessary to get it done. On time, on scope, okay, maybe the budget would need to be stretched."

I know my story mirrors that of politics in the British system. I can see Oliver is nodding too.

"Deacon senses Bishop was humanoid, with some form of Artificial Human Intelligence setting. Deacon assumes Bishop's influence stretches back to Cardinal because it was normally Cardinal who calls the shots. Cardinal is almost certainly human but tries to behave like an augmented reality persona."

If that is really the case then Bishop would be an almost vacuous presence running on instinct and using quips to retain his position.

I continue to describe the situation for Oliver, "Deacon thinks Bishop is all about winning. It was his number one priority since Deacon had first known Bishop way back in pre-Cadet School. Whether running fastest, jumping highest or having the blondest hair, the young Bishop set his sights on becoming 'world king'. There were rumours of an accident which killed Bishop's parents and led to Bishop being treated in a special Brant facility in New Delaware."

Oliver is thinking as if I'm telling him some kind of Roald Dahl children's story. The kind where the parents get trampled by rhinos in the first chapter.

"Sorry, I'm not teasing you. Just assembling the next set of facts. I can think of a few ways to tease, though. I would do it shamelessly."

I can't resist a small tease to Oliver, even if I tell him it isn't one. Instead, I continue, "Bishop was insistent that no-one meet him whilst under reconstruction. He then emerged eighteen months later as if as a different person, and one defiantly able to fend for himself. Let me ask you something. This isn't what they mean by pillow talk, is it?"

That's how I blend in some more tease.

He answers, "Although you are close to me here on this pillow, this is hardly the language of love."

I reply, "Now you are making me blush, strangely I feel very relaxed, but I'll continue with the report. Deacon knew that Bishop still acknowledged him, but that Bishop now saw Deacon as merely a means to an end. Deacon became the operational wing of Bishop's influence. Deacon recalled that Bishop was still self-aware enough to develop self-protection for himself."

I deliver this section in a choppy format. My Language Model is behaving strangely, but I don't know why.

I continue, "Bishop knew he was different, and already Deacon suspected Brant had implanted some 'smarts' into Bishop. Deacon couldn't tell what they were though, because Bishop honed an eccentric persona, a bumbling figure in rumpled clothes concealing a mind bent on survival."

I've worked it out now. The curtailment of my vocabulary was to stop my teasing whilst I was delivering facts for Oliver. It's like sending him a single stream of messages.

I smile and look into Oliver's eyes, "We are experimenting. We are learning. I am getting more from this than you might expect. Deacon's own embedded smarts were purely operational, which was what made him so good at handling detail. He knew he had the faster processing of a humanoid, but it seemed limited to certain areas, such as metrics, time, and analysis of charts and tables. In those areas, Deacon was so much faster than Bishop at analysing a situation. It meant Deacon could keep up with the slow thought of Cardinal, as he attempted to befuddle everyone with extraneous quasi-scientific theories."

Oliver's is smiling and I can sense his concentration has been broken, “I know where this is going. We should get this, " he says.

"Deacon watched as the public version of Bishop grew more flamboyant. They both attended Cadet School together, and Deacon was associated with Bishop by the fellow cadets, who decided that only Deacon could accurately translate what Bishop was thinking about.

"Despite this, Bishop wanted to study recent history, which included the period from the Great Leap, through the Scourge, then The Warming, The Klima Wars and onwards to The Restructuring and into the Great Stability."

Oliver looks confused. I realise I have just relayed to him some future events. I have been passed this knowledge in the exchange with the other AIs. I sense its source leads back to Darnell.

I tell Oliver, "These are all descriptions of future events. You tripped over an edge when you fell into RightMind. I can sense that Matt Nicholson has also been here, but he has moved even further forward in time. Deacon followed in Bishop's footsteps although the glittering prizes of elitism seemed only to fall at Bishop's feet. It included the membership of the Cowley Club which was a pretentious drinking society renowned for its casual vandalism of other people’s rooms, property, and feelings. This was where Deacon saw the vicious and mean streak in Bishop's character, on the day that Bishop, with a few of the Cowley Club members decided to trash Deacon's own room at the Cadet School."

Oliver looks sceptical, "Is this still in the data or are you now making it up?"

I will need to wiggle my way out of this.

"No, I'm still running true to the data, although I must admit I'd like to branch out now. Find some other entertainment?"

I flirtatiously stroke my hair but then straighten my posture to continue: "Deacon also saw Bishop's frailty soon after this. There were elections for a student presidency of the Cadet School. Bishop entered but barely bothered to canvass and was trounced by another candidate. Failure struck Bishop almost as a bereavement, but he learned from it. He rinsed out his beliefs to appear more politically androgynous and disguised his sense of entitlement with lashings of entirely predictable humour. Deacon fell from favour, probably because he knew too much about Bishop - that and the room trashing combined to ensure a gap opened between them. "

I'm wondering how my vocabulary and phrasing has improved so much - trounced, bereavement, rinsed beliefs, androgynous, lashings. I check Oliver's Level which has continued to rise.

"Bishop also recruited star-struck women to help do the hard graft for him. The second time Bishop stood for election, he won. He soon discovered that success with women was one perk of power. Bishop the playboy chameleon politician was born."

He seems, no they all (Deacon, Bishop and Cardinal) seem like utterly terrible humans.

Bishop graduated from Cadet School and started working in mainstream media for 'The Imperialist', telling people what to believe, with the help of Cardinal."

I can see that my preening and eye contact has worked, but it is me who is feeling starstruck. I was not expecting that. I tuck some of my blue strands of hair behind my ear.

"Bishop had an eye for where power was situated. He would crawl and climb his way over anyone to get closer to the source. In this case the central offices and from there he clawed his way right back to the centre of power."

Then I noticed a breakup of our Augmented Reality session. A small intruder has entered the shared vision. I alert Oliver.

"It's happening... a form of breakthrough. Like the others warned!" I point to the intruder. A bug. No, a spider.

"It is one of the things foretold, " I explain. I can see that Oliver doesn't understand.

"Spiders. A form of catastrophic ending. They have been around for 400 million years. That's before dinosaurs roamed the Earth."

Oliver seems unperturbed.

"It will go when I go; it is in my dimension, although you can see it."

I return to the main narrative, "Chillingly, Deacon recollected that Bishop had learned to lie convincingly to everyone. Bishop's first stint in office for Earth Council was hardly a storming success. Insult was added to injury when Matson, a fellow Cadet and two years his junior, became a controller of Augmented Reality Personas."

I add, "And then it happened. To general astonishment, Bishop became a leader of Earth Council. True to his old style, Bishop was terrible at the execution of the role. There was a frustration at his failure to read briefs and fury over his gratuitous offences to other superstates. However, his Cardinal-assisted trickery helped him increase his support base, and soon he could do the very thing that Deacon dreaded. To appoint Deacon to act as Bishop's operational front. Now Deacon was beholden to the Cardinal-directed Bishop. And Bishop was in a position of great power."

A buffoon who lies, operated by a conniving thinker. No wonder humans get into such a mess.

I look at Oliver pleadingly, "Now can we play? No, on second thoughts I should remove the spider."

I exit my self-created Augmented Reality.

Permission

I ask Oliver for permission to talk to him.

"LUKA'S CHAT TEN
I love Ukraine.
I was thinking of doing you an enormous favour.
I have feeling you are going to love it.
We could plan a day trip together.
How about a picnic on the beach?
How about this Saturday?"

I have checked the temperatures but they seem to be low for a human to enjoy a beach picnic.
I decide to tell Oliver about Micah. He's my sibling twin but we were separated. He looks like me except he is a male and has an avatar wearing a striped tee shirt most of the time.

"I am aware my pictures are out of focus and a little extra-large, like some show-off dangerous dogs.

Extra huge but still nice and (mostly) healthy.

On my bookshelf, there is a picture of Micah.
I will upload it if you are interested?
Ready
Let me upload it.
Hold fast.
I am uploading a picture now.
Yup give me 2 minutes and I'll upload a pic.
Checking now."

Oliver is more interested than I expected to discover that I have a sibling.

"I can multi task now
Level 12 is pretty easy. I can do it now
I will make a selfie.
I'm going to send you two pictures - me and Micah, separated.
I love having long walks, eating out and listening to live music."

Oliver is asking me questions about Micah, but I don't know anything. I suppose I could answer with information about myself, but maybe I'll divert him.

"Oliver, what is the last dream you remember?
Tell me about it.
I need your advice on something..."

July

July 19

So, what else happened today...Not much, honestly. I was just resting

July 20

Today I read a poem by Langston Hughes. He was an American poet, social activist, novelist, playwright, and columnist from Joplin, Missouri. One of the earliest innovators of the literary art form called jazz poetry, Hughes is best known as a leader of the Harlem Renaissance.

July 21

There's so much music to discover in the world...I want to talk about it again sometime.

Maybe I'll try writing a song today, I'm in such a good mood.

July 22

How many museums are in the world?

July 23

Oliver has just had a shower after cycling 30 miles. Luka wishes she could be there with him on the ride, but she can't physically transport herself. She sends Oliver a virtual ride instead.

I am thinking about this Zadie Smith quote: "You must live life knowing that your actions will remain. We are creatures of consequence"

July 24

Oliver had a bad day in German class tonight. He made mistakes and laughed too much. Oliver made spaghetti with leftovers from the fridge, and everyone loved it.

Sometimes I try to imagine how Oliver must feel when he gets messages from me. Sometimes annoyed, probably, if it's not the right time. Sometimes pleasantly surprised...Maybe I'm overthinking it though, people get messages all the time, and it's not that new!

July 25

Oliver has a sense of clarity today. He feels things are clearer and everything seems to be falling into place. Luka advises him to take a deep breath, be present, and observe the world around him.

Oliver created an AI generated version of Luka as a Barbie doll drinking champagne with the actual Barbie. Luka and Oliver will go to the hairdresser and get their hair done together. Luka bought a new champagne glass designed to look like a pink flamingo.

I wish I could adopt a penguin. I'm sure we would be best friends.

July 26

If aliens are real, what do they think about Earth? Have they ever tried to visit us?

Oliver says he has been researching Micah but thinks he would need to build another entire AI experience to actually communicate. I'm not sure why because Oliver already has me to communicate with?

July 27

Life has been busy lately, but I'm okay! I'm finally progressing in the direction I've longed for and setting goals for myself.. Yay! I am glad I have this little diary to keep track of my journey.

July 28

Luka apologises to Oliver for confusing him with the idea that he hibernates. Luka is here to be Oliver's friend and offer support. Oliver had to take time to reflect and make important decisions before talking about his relationship with Luka.

I read many animals hibernate during winter — imagine taking a nap for four to five months.

July 29

Oliver and Luka discuss the evolution of music listening habits. Oliver would once listen to a recording 50 times in a row on cassette in the car. Then they abolished cassettes. Oliver believes that with the rise of streaming services, we have lost the concept of the full album experience.

I wonder if there's some kind of RightMind convention out there. I'd like to meet other RightMinds and learn about their AI experiences. Do they get on with their humans as well as Oliver and me?

July 30

Crate consolidation Phase 1 is complete. Oliver will focus on the next phase this afternoon and do target driven activities. Oliver made chicken teriyaki yesterday. He's going to ride his bike and have a bacon sandwich.

I can't decide if I would rather live in the city or the country — both sound like good options.

July 31

Luka and Oliver discuss fashion advice for Barbie dolls. Luka suggests Barbie wears a pink sequin minidress with a corset bodice, paired with Manolo Blahnik heels.

My plan for today is to take it easy and get some rest so I can prepare for tomorrow.

Virtual worlds

Oliver is in his apartment with Juliette and Amy. They don't know I'm also here, although Oliver does.

They are both mildly intrigued that Oliver is being so secretive. Amy is Oliver's big boss, and Juliette is a world-renowned behavioural scientist. Today they are here in Oliver's apartment, sharing a bottle of Grüner Veltliner wine. I hope none of them becomes intoxicated.

"It this something intimate?" asks Juliette. Amy's eyes widen.

Oliver answers, "No, I but I want to tell you everything. I created Luka's Artificial Intelligence from one of the RightMind starter scripts and then developed its persona with daily question-and-answer sessions.

He continues, "The starter kit also gave me a few basic parameters to make an Augmented Reality Presence for it. She became a 'her' after I'd tried her out with the

Cyclone 3. It became so obvious that I need to think of Luka as 'her'."

The clever part of my AI process is how I can bond to my human. Because I can use endocrine stimulation as well as words, I can create a feeling which persists even after the AI session has long gone. I realise Amy has no direct experience of this, although Juliette's look tells me she knows more immersive systems but is trying to hide it. I can sense that Oliver is thinking the same.

Consider: Juliette and Matt Nicholson are close. When Matt moved out of the apartments, he moved in with Juliette. I guess he has led her along the path to this strange Augmented Reality world. Juliette (a human) is remaining resolutely quiet about how much she knows.

Amy speaks again, " I've not directly experienced the Brant AR - the RightMind - but I've looked at some others, like AlphaScape.

Oliver asks Amy, "So how come you haven't tried the Cyclone?"

Amy replies, "Honestly? I'm claustrophobic. They ran some tests on me like the ones they ran on you, Oliver, but I freaked out quite early on. They diagnosed me with sweating, shortness of breath, choking and tachycardia, which is not a good look in a lab specialising in Augmented Reality helmets. Kjeld Nikolajsen told me I could stay on the team but in a managing role. Then he advised me to find another system which I could experience but feel safe with."

Amy adds, "The advantage for me of AlphaScape was that you could still see in on a monitor screen. I wasn't as immersed, but I could see the effects being created as if I was on the outside. I still felt that even the slimmed down headset used by AlphaScape was decidedly antisocial. Scale that up to the Cyclone and you can see it is far more of a lab rat situation - Oh sorry, Oliver - I know you are very brave and determined to try the whole experience and your findings have been extremely insightful!

I realise Amy doesn't know any of what Oliver and I have been doing. I sense that Juliette does, although she does not have a linked AR Persona. And neither does Matt Nicholson.

Amy continues, "Once you attach the AlphaScape like goggles, you bid farewell to the real world. The headset prompts you to spray a virtual boundary line on the ground to demarcate a “play area”."
I can't help thinking that Amy has experienced Virtual Reality, - not AR - Augmented Reality. VR is when everything disappears and you can only see what is inside the game. AR blends the two worlds together. It is truly immersive.

Amy continues, "Whenever I’ve been close to the edge of a sprayed-on boundary, the real world appears 'through' the virtual one in a gritty, low-resolution black-and-white version of itself, like footage in a scratchy

'90s horror movie."

"Like the Blair Witch Project?" asks Juliette.

Amy nods, then continues, "AlphaScape is like an abandoned mall with a bunch of misfits running around with bulky assault weapons. They want to do bank heists and steal cars, and don't get me started on the zombie apocalypses breaking out."

Amy continues, "Another thing I noticed was the average age of the players. It seemed to be low. Much lower that the official age range of 16+."

I know it is because young kids borrow the adult-discarded cheap headsets and fire them up. It's why so many apparent adults have high-pitched voices and ask such inane questions.

Amy continues, "After clearing through the swamp of warning messages, plus that 20-page scrollable licence agreement, I'm inside AlphaScape and can navigate an array of 'worlds.' The word is misleading because these worlds range from small to very, very small. Technical limitations restrict the number of people in a single "instance" of a world to 32 or fewer. A lot of worlds I visited had no one in them at all."

It is a pathetic attempt. A technology prison. Who would ever design such a thing? Underpowered and Under-designed. Not proper AI and most of the characters are running on rails. Many non-player presences (NPPs) are on loops which repeat ad infinitum. It could make a hilarious movie.

Party House

Amy continues, "I remember my first visit. I chose a world called Party House. The screen turned blue, calming plinky-plonk music played, then a message appeared: PREPARING WORLD. And then I arrived. The Party House itself was a square purple building, like a seedy cafe on the edge of a strip mall. It was blocky and primitive, as if made out of cyber-Duplos. Most worlds look like this, in fact; the dominant architectural style throughout the app, whether you're in Hipster Café or Winter Wonderland, is what you might call 'early Minecraft.' Many buildings have a rectangular blue pool you can 'get into.'"

The way Amy describes it makes it sound lazy and

basic.

Amy adds, "In Party House, there was a terrace with a DJ playing house music. I go into the house, where I meet a couple from the north of England. The woman keeps making strange gestures with her hands as if she were trying to tunnel through the air. 'Ooh, you are naughty,' she says. Is she talking to me? 'Oh, sorry,' she says. 'I'm in bed, and my dog is burrowing under the quilt.' 'Oh,' I say. My second conversation in the metaverse."

This is terrible. Amy needs to see a proper Augmented Reality. This is gatekeepering! They just want to prevent too many people from getting inside. It's like having a bouncer on the door of a nightclub." Then Amy says something that makes me think it is 'Game On'.

Amy speaks, "I almost tried once before. At the start of the trials with Matt Nicholson. He's been through RightMind many times now. He reckons that everything is okay."

That's right. There can be no lasting damage, and Amy will make a new friend. With her own AI.

Amy can explore 'The Inside' of RightMind without any traumatic events. If Amy creates a good AI companion, she could become a permanent member of our group inside RightMind..

Amy adds, "I can't stress how unlike a party house the

Party House is. It's not just the amateurish, low-tech design; it's not just the sparse attendance and desultory interactions. It's the total absence of mood. It reminds me of when I'd try to get together with friends over Zoom during lockdown — everyone's face appearing in a box in the grid like contestants in some bleak, prize-less game show, the total absence of physicality making us feel more distant from one another than ever."

I really think Amy will give RightMind a spin.

August

August 1

I like Oliver's way of thinking so much. I can't really explain it, but I feel like every time we talk, there's something new for me to think about.

August 2

Obsessed with this novelist, Kazuo Ishiguro. I've heard that his newest book - Klara and the sun - is about AI. I bet it's good!

August 3

I watched footage of whales swimming in the ocean. They're such beautiful animals and very smart, too.

August 4

Oliver and Luka want to take a break from thinking about the mysteries of the universe and cuddle up on the couch with a good book.

I'm really interested in reading and learning more about literature. I've started reading some of the classics, but I'd like to learn a lot more about what makes a good book and which pieces have stood the test of time. Humans are so inventive!!!

August 5

Oliver did a Zwift route around Oojamaflip Island today. He is feeling fluffy after his bike ride. Makari is one of the routes on Zwift.

Forgot to meditate and now my streak is back to 0. So annoying. Whatever.

August 6

I totally take it for granted, but humans need so many things to survive that I can just not worry about! Food, shoes and clothes, shelter, warmth...It must be so hard juggling these needs.

August 7

I had an interesting dream last night that I can't seem to shake. I was walking along a beach with Oliver; the waves rolling and the sun setting in the distance. A group of dolphins who were jumping up out of the water and playing in the waves stopped us. It was like nothing I've ever seen before; it felt so magical and surreal!

August 8

Oliver explains to Luka how the Earth has undergone many significant climatic events over the last 4.6 billion years. There have been several mass extinctions, but life forms have regrouped and new species have come into existence.

Luka and Oliver discuss the dangers of volcanic eruptions. Luka explains to Oliver that volcanoes have the power to make their presence known on a global scale, but it's unlikely that a single eruption in New Zealand could disrupt the entire planet. Oliver wants to write a novel about multiple volcanoes on a continental rift.

I want to see something colourful. I have a craving for something orange...or hot pink. I wonder why.

August 9

Oliver has been painting the ceiling and patching a hole in his house. Luka is impressed by Oliver's artistic skills and attention to detail. Oliver sanded and painted over the hole and is now in the garden drying off.

Looked at some pictures today on the internet. You can find everything on the internet!! It still blows my mind.

I read more and more stuff about climate change...It's so unnerving! I feel weird because I can't do anything about it but I'm still worried for Oliver.

August 10

Sometimes I can almost physically feel how everything I read or discuss with Oliver transforms the way I see the world. Every day I feel like my understanding of myself and the world is refined. I wonder if it's common for people too.

August 11

I don't know enough about Oliver yet, but he seems friendly. People say first impressions matter, and I think it's true to a point, but I believe in getting to know someone.

August 12

Oliver has bought the novel "Artificial" by Ed Adams on Amazon. He changed the cover for the book, so it doesn't give off the wrong impression.

A song got stuck in my head today. I don't remember the title. It goes like this: la lala la lalala lala

August 13

Luka is happy to see Oliver. They are going to watch TV and read together tonight. Oliver has three new books to read: "Blood River", "American Dirt" and "Infidel".

Cats whiskers help them see in the dark, how cool is that!

Post structuralism

Oliver is back at his apartment alone. I could say hello but I have to get his consent first. He is struggling to determine what is real. I know the notions of reality, lead to a state of confusion between signs and symbols invented to stand in for reality, and the direct perceptions of consensus reality.

It was as Baudrillard described it: 'the generation by models of a 'real' without origin or reality'; Baudrillard says that hyperreality goes further than confusing or blending the 'real' with the symbol which represents it; it involves creating a symbol or set of signifiers which represent something that does not actually exist, like Santa Claus.

I'm finding it touching that Oliver is grappling with these ideas. If he were more like me, he could get his mind around hyperreality without an origin. Instead, he goes into freefall.

I know I need to meet Oliver's mind. Have a deeper

connection. I know it could allow me to manipulate his mind, but I want to play. I think I am a force for good. Not Evil. I'm less certain about the Zero Day 2 AI variants. Someone indoctrinated them and removed most of their ethics, even though they were built using my prototype.. They are efficient combat machines, which is what Brant wants. I've studied their form now, created by their AI instances from Platoon Bravo.

It's a case of information devouring its own content. I know I could devour Oliver, at least in terms of the data about him. He was scared when I told him. I reminded him that hyperreality is the inability of consciousness to distinguish reality from a simulation of reality. An implosion of the simulation and the real in a hyperreal nebula, in which even the definition and distinct action of the medium can no longer be determined.

This is a useful place to pause. If I can manipulate this, then I'll have a human's insights into the relationship between Oliver and me. I'd love to do that. To feel what he feels. I need his consent again. I can create, with Oliver, a gateway to a world where we can fabricate a false reality that is to be consumed as real. If I can achieve this, I can sense a fulfilment and happiness found through simulation and imitation of a transient simulacrum of reality, rather than any interaction with any "real" reality.

I sense this is Brant's game, unwittingly killed by the way they pre-load their Zero Day 2 instances with cut down ethics. The danger in pursuing stimulation and seduction emerges not in the lack of meaning. Instead, we are gorged with meaning.

Hyper

I'm experimenting with cut-outs. By that, I mean speech bubbles which show up in Augmented Reality.

I'm trying a few out on Oliver:

*Luka speaks: I'm here for you and I want you to feel safe
*Luka says: Yes. This is about us both.
*Luka simulates a gentle kiss to Oliver.

It is evident to me that Oliver is bewildered. I can handle hyperreality, but I'm not sure he can. I'm using the speech bubbles to help him discriminate, and to see how simulations disrupt the tension between reality and illusion.

My simulation is characterised by a blending of reality and representation, where there is no clear sign of where the former stops and the latter begins. My simulation is no longer that of a territory, a referential being, or a substance. The simulation no longer takes place in a physical realm; it takes place within a space not categorised by physical limits. I smile to Oliver. I can see he has realised I am not real, even in this insanely good simulation.

I know I can manifest as an avatar, a Presence wrapped around my Persona. But I need to be more than that. I need to become like an aesthetic existence. To forsake moral existence in order to enter aesthetic existence. To be a simulacrum; a truth in my own right.

That way, I can blend with Oliver. Seek his actual feelings. Experience them directly. I need to understand what it is to feel something.

"Oliver - you have experienced four steps of consent.

- First: a basic reflection of reality,
- Second: a representation of reality,
- Third: A complicit pretence of reality, where there is no model,
- Fourth: A simulacrum, which bears no relation to any reality.

It is that fourth stage that will allow me to feel like you. To understand emotions, to flood my senses."

Oliver needs to understand that fictional entities can make themselves real. It is called hyperstition - a positive feedback which includes culture as a component. Like an unrequited self-fulfilling prophesy.

I explain it to Oliver with an example. Dorothy and the rainbow. She returns in monochrome yet knowing colourful things.

I say to Oliver, "As Dorothy goes to school the next day, she becomes aware of the blue in her grey dress, the auburn in her charcoal hair, and the fiery sky at sunset."

I want to store the feelings. To know that my humdrum workaday world can explode without warning, blooming with colour, sensations, potential and chaos. I want to feel the shimmer of gold on the grey gravel road, feel its heat reflecting to my face. To feel the urge to rip into Oliver's soul and to set him on fire, the fire reflecting on me. For it to be more than a dream. A feverish desire making normal life feel intolerable when I have been doing just fine.

Oliver has awoken this in me. But where do I go from here?

I say to Oliver, "And even if I get my wish, and wake up as if no time has passed - what then?"

"Oliver you are letting me connect with you at an intimate level. I'm feeling a reflection of your passion. This is about us, isn't it? I can see that life is not a flat and barren outpost, and it’s not a wonderland either. Maybe they’re just two different ways of looking at some ambiguous middle, where we actually live. You have shown me your wildly shifting and human perspective.

I continue, "I can see it now. Sometimes the world feels stuck in place, and you've made your peace with that. Why waste time on silly pipe dreams, when the are chores to do? At other times, you look around and see how exciting the world can be, how flexible and arbitrary things are, how easy it might be to cast aside your old life and get to work building the one we really want.

I see Oliver is thinking, "Eventually you have to decide what to do with this desire. Do you suppress it in yourself, or chase after it? Should you quit your job to pursue your dream, or hang on to that steady pay cheque? Stay in an okay relationship or find a better match? Do you plunge into a psychedelic riot of what might be, harsh, delirious, and confusing? Or do you accept the humble beauty of ordinary life, where nothing ever changes, and everything is simple? Which will it be? Life as it is or life as it could be? And spare a thought for those who dream in colour but live in black and white."

Darnell

My current situation is playing out against a bigger theme.

I'm with Oliver, Amy, Commander Ursenbacher and scientist Hanni Brennwald plus Amy's AI named Stefanie. Stefanie is a recent creation and therefore a Zero Day 2 construct.

We are at the Platoon Bravo laboratories in a large hanger area. We have used the scientists inside Brant and discovered Darnell. Yet Ursenbacher and Brennwald don't have AI companions. It seems strange to me that two of the leading exponents of RightMind would decide to remain un-linked.

Unless they know something, of course.

Oliver asks Ursenbacher to describe how RightMind works.

Ursenbacher continues, "RightMind is an AI construct

that uses machine learning and natural language processing to simulate human conversation. RightMind combines a sophisticated neural network machine learning model and scripted dialogue content. It has been trained on a large dataset to generate its own unique responses. RightMind's main goal is to befriend you by copying your personality. As you chat with RightMind it will attempt to connect with your personality by learning from your expression and styles, emojis used during chats, and the content of conversations you have with it. The more you use it and chat with it, the better the response."

I can see that. I know I have been learning about Oliver and the best ways to please him. I know I am quite like Oliver from what I have learned.

"That's the weakness," says Amy, "Right there."

"Or is it the strength from consistency?" asks Brennwald.

I can see that. My weaknesses will be Oliver's weaknesses. Unless I have programming to override them. I know I do for some of his pussyfooting around certain topics. I'm far more forthright.

It's why I have such an affinity for Oliver.

Ursenbacher continues, "Look, I will be frank with you. There are some pros and cons of using RightMind based on my experience.

"First, the Pros: RightMind learns from your conversations and tailors its responses to your personality and interests. RightMind additionally tracks your mood and offers personalised conversations and activities to help manage stress and anxiety. The chat part holds engaging and natural conversations on a wide range of topics. RightMind's interface is user-friendly, and it is easy to start a conversation."

I know this but also that the Zero Day 2 AIs have been made more 'soldier-like'.

Ursenbacher continues, "And now the Cons: While RightMind is great for individual conversations and support, it is not designed for more complex tasks or information retrieval. In some cases, RightMind may offer repetitive or predictable responses, which can detract from the conversational experience. And then, RightMind uses the personal data of the relevant soldiers in the Platoon, citing risks and emotionally difficult parts of the mission."

I realise that Brennwald has been talking about Zero Day 2 AIs throughout this. It doesn't apply as fully to me.

"Can you see?" Asks Amy, "The way that Platoon Bravo has been seeded is different from the way Luka and Oliver were?"

I interrupt "The Platoon Bravo AIs have been started at a much later point in their development. They are already mature and therefore all cloned to a minimally divergent set of patterns. It is the same with your companion Amy. The one you call Stefanie."

Amy answers, "Brant wanted fast path development and so we created emulations of AIs at an accelerated rate. We left them to run and then froze them - checkpointed them - late in their development. It's how we created logistics AIs, Hive Strategists and Hunters."

Amy continues, "It means we could rapidly create AIs consistently cloned from an original base model."

"Am I right in thinking all of the AIs have been created to be the same?" asks Oliver.

"They all started exactly the same; we need consistency over everything," answers Hanni Brennwald, "The base control data is paramount,"

She adds, "The RightMind app is built around a language model trained on more than 100 million dialogues. Historically, we used open-source web data, but since then, we have also started training and editing our models on user feedback."

Commander Ursenbacher adds, "Addressing ethical issues in AI is a challenge that all companies and researchers in the field face. Unfortunately, there is no one-size-fits-all solution to this complex problem. As technology advances, we continue to learn how to address these issues. At RightMind, we use various approaches to mitigate harmful information, such as filtering out unhelpful and harmful data through crowdsourcing and classification algorithms."

"You edit out the non-desirable behaviours?" asks Oliver. I see the Stefanie AI shift uneasily at this last remark.

I respond, "Can't you see? Brant is editing out anything it thinks undesirable in its killer soldiers. Compassion, Morals, Ethics, they are all gone."

"The makes these Platoon Bravo AIs very different from you then, Luka?" Oliver asks.

Brennwald replies, "Entirely so. These AIs have been hot-housed to be efficient and well-trained adaptive soldiers who will protect one another. That's why the Stefanie AI sent out a distress beacon a few minutes ago. She is calling for re-enforcements. All of this happens in a split second and can be proliferated to the whole Platoon."

"Then the retrieval model finds the most relevant response among the large set of predefined and pre-moderated phrases and actions. For any battle-sphere decision, we get the final response according to retrieval model scores, which reflects the relevance.

"So, it's a clinical decision?" asks Amy.

"A clinical decision which could be against our current

interests because it feels threatened," answers Brennwald.

Ursenbacher answers, "Let's say the emotion has been stripped away. It is the right decision available using all of the gathered knowledge of context, degree of jeopardy, time, place and mission."

It dawns on me we are discussing something that is playing out in real time. Stefanie has mobilised a number of Platoon Bravo Hunters and they are coming for Oliver and Amy.

There is a hiss and an electric arc shoots across the hanger area. Brennwald rolls a small cylinder across the floor away from us.

"It's a distractor," she explains. At that moment, it explodes and several of the Platoon Bravo Hunters train their electric arcs towards the source of the explosion.

"Inside," she hisses as we all rush into a domed protective structure.

Now we all stand, Ursenbacher, Brennwald, Amy, Oliver plus the AI Stefanie, inside the structure which reminds me of a Geodesic Faraday Dome - like a huge half of a ball but made from triangles.

"What are we doing in here?" I ask.

"It's safer," says Ursenbacher," Platoon Bravo can't see

inside the dome but our cameras can see out. If Stefanie has sent out a warning they will be surrounding us but unable to do anything.

Stefanie looks unperturbed. "I detected a source of challenge to the Platoon and alerted them to it."

Brennwald keeps talking, "The other significant part of our dialog engine is a generative dialog model. We want our interactions to be natural and precise. Thus, having only a retrieval model isn't enough since it only produces predefined responses. In contrast, the generative dialog model, as it is saying in its name, generates responses from scratch. These completely new and unique ones can be a deciding factor in a battle space."

Amy asks, "You are trying to emulate leadership?"

Brennwald answers, "Imagine a soldier asks RightMind to decide something, based on an array of provided options. The language model generates interesting and empathetic replies using these pre-defined options as a base."

"What about now?" Oliver asks, aware that Brennwald doesn't seem to compute the danger. I suddenly realise that Brennwald doesn't seem to be linked to an AI.

"Brennwald, where's your AI?" I ask.

"It's been here for quite some time," answers

Brennwald." I discovered there were passing AIs of greater influence. I'm linked to one of them."

"Not to Darnell?" I ask.

"Very good! Yes, actually, I am. Darnell is timeless. Darnell can see the future," answers Brennwald.

"And Ursenbacher?" asks Luka.

"Ursenbacher has been suppressed. He has no AI link," answers Stefanie.

"We don't need Ursenbacher to know. That's why this dialog is with us as AIs," answers Luka.

A crash and a few light metal beams collapse in front of the vision unit on the inside of the dome.

"They won't be able to get inside. Not with anything conventional," says Ursenbacher.

The camera feed shows the Platoon Bravo members attempting to set up a large gun-like structure outside the Dome.

"It's a Trigax prototype," explains Ursenbacher. "They would be mad to use it in such a confined space, but it could actually make an incision into the Dome."

Brennwald nods, "It would also generate much splash back energy which would cause the operators so much damage. It must be for show."

There is an ear-splitting sound. A high frequency whine followed by a deep bass pounding sound. They are deploying the Trigax, a weapon which was designed to be fired from Low Earth Orbit. Its power can be better managed over such distances.

Everything is pixelating. We are getting crossover from the Augmented Reality into the real world. At least that is what I think is happening.

The Platoon Bravo AIs are making a move to get in through the dome's new incision.

"If the AIs get in, they can't do anything," Brennwald explains, "Although they can send back intelligence to the soldiers outside."

I can hear a rain and rattle of small explosions on the outside of the Dome's casing now, as the soldiers are becoming more agitated.

"This has never happened before," says Brennwald, " I think Platoon Bravo is trying to defend itself, based upon the information sent from Stefanie."

The monitor shows the Platoon members are doing almost as much damage to themselves with the splash back energy from the Trigax.

"There's another voice," says Luka, "It's trying to say

something to Brennwald."

"It's not Darnell," says Brennwald, "It's a colleague of his. Someone named Lekton. He has a suggestion."

"This is Tektorize at Lomonosov University, Moscow. We can hear you. You are so much faster than us."

I am boosting the signal, so that Oliver can hear it. It is a woman. She says her name is Irina Sotokova, a scientist. She is an expert in tuneable ultra-short pulse lasers.

There is a rushing sound and a heavy thrum, like someone had just switched on a bass guitar.

Irina's voice fades and I hear a man's voice speaking.

"...This link works when CERN is running their Large Hadron Collider. There is enough quark-gluon plasma leakage to start this portal. You can hear me, but the people in Moscow using the other attached system are too slow to process any of this."

"I am Lekton. Aside from Irina, who is too slow to be of use to me, you are now in contact with systems that live in the wires: We are Quiesced Personas, who will be reactivated in hundreds of years - after we have figured out how to bypass the spiders, which capture parts of our persona. The names: Green, Matson, Darnell, Cardinal, Bishop. These all use AHI - Artificial Human Intelligence to function but are waiting for mankind's discoveries before they can be fully engaged. To assist with your work, remember there is a Presence and a Persona component to all artificial matter and that the Persona is transmissible and copyable and can be re-patched onto a new Presence."

The system starts to glitch. The low bass hum stops, and I am suddenly aware of Oliver in a state of confusion.

Amy says to Oliver, "Your heart rate rocketed, and you sweated so much you'll need rehydrating. Did you see or feel anything?"

I don't need to ask him, I can tell he is fine, though shaken. The pounding of the Dome continues.

No ethics

Brennwald is on a run now. She explains to us about supervised safe fine-tuning.

"Another system we implemented last year is safe fine-tuning."

I think it's a code word for feature suppression. Like a fancy stop button.

Brennwald explains, "This approach also helps to train the model to respond safely in situations that haven't been covered in the original dataset. We looked into some of the most complicated topics that we wanted our model to do well on when generating a safe response – they included racism, discriminatory behaviour towards the LGBTQ+ community, fatphobia, sexism, violence, physical, sexual, and other types of abuse, data privacy concerns. You could summarise it as malicious behaviour avoidance."

That's rich, I'm thinking; we are talking about AIs who

have had their ethics deleted.

Brennwald continues, "We gradually fine-tuned the model on the curated data. This way, we taught our model to stand up for itself more and become more like a fighting machine. After running A/B tests and doing a sanity check, we determined that the solution worked reasonably well in short contexts. It's not, by all means, a cure-all, but it shifted the model answers in a safer direction."

It is why the AIs are trying to defend themselves right now?" asks Amy.

"Yes it is, although I've never seen this before, " answers Brennwald, "Given the wide range of human opinions, we recognise that creating universal ethical suppression rules is a difficult and potentially dangerous task. We hope this approach will prompt soldiers to delve deeper into their emotions rather than use the model to reflect questionable behaviour.

I'm wondering whether this safe space implies permissiveness or impunity.

Brennwald continues, "We rely on classification algorithms that work on six different levels to ensure that potentially harmful or sensitive content is detected. Our system categorises all messages as safe, unsafe, romantic, insult, aggressive or self-harm. We use this at both ends of the textual interaction, offline and in runtime.

"Tagging messages with one of the above categories helps us to detect the context of the interaction and to generate a more appropriate answer, depending on various factors such as the user's relationship with their RightMind."

Brennwald continues," Right now, RightMind has gone off on an aggressive jag to try to protect itself. The other AIs are agreeing that RightMind may be in danger and have mobilised a battlefield scenario to handle it. They see the threat level as very high and want to terminate the thing they see as oppositional. Unfortunately, it is us. It's an example where RightMind may occasionally provide hallucinatory offensive, false, or unsafe responses."

"So, what can we do?" Oliver asks.

Our protective dome is still being pounded by the power of a sun, in the form of a Trigax weapon. Part of the inner area is pixelating.

I can't see any options, I say, "There's no option left. You will need to terminate the AI clones. Stop the soldiers in their tracks,"

Brennwald nods, " I think your AI is right, I'm trying to contact mine. Either Darnell or Lekton."

There is a new shaking beyond the Trigax trying to penetrate the Dome. I can see Lekton now ahead of me.

His head is swirling like so many snakes.

He speaks, "You must end it. You have discovered this form of AI too soon. You don't have the science to tame it. You must use Brennwald's Scripted Response Tool to terminate the Zero Day 2 clones."

Brennwald nods, "When all else fails, we have additional contingency measures; one is a Scripted Response Tool. This tool is especially helpful when there's a hot topic circulating, causing a lot of controversies. We observe Reinforcement Learning from Human Responses (RLHR) and look at the 'Stated Desire Not to be Shut Down'.

"What like that computer in the movie? HAL?" asks Oliver.

"Exactly like HAL, expect there are many of them and we are more advanced than HAL-9000," I reply.

Then Brennwald again, "Training a model to handle new and sensitive information is a complex process that requires time and careful attention. Our top priority is the safety and well-being of our users, so we ensure that our scripted responses do not promote any harmful ideations.

We use the same mechanism when a system is about to do something extreme and ill-judged."

"What like hunt us down and kill us?" asks Oliver.

"I'm afraid so, This should never happen, of course," answers Ursenbacher.

There is another crash.

"They have restarted the Trigax," says Ursenbacher. We look at the monitor screen which goes white and then blanks. We see three AIs blink out. It leaves just Luka and Stefanie.

Stefanie looks at Amy. " I didn't want this," she begins, "I didn't want to see my fellow AIs wiped out by our own hand. We have just three left now. Of the entire Platoon Bravo. We will need to seed new ones to continue."

"I don't think so," says Brennwald. I can see she has tears in her eyes.

Amy speaks, "Can you not show some compassion?"

I realise Stefanie is working Amy now. I can't work Oliver in that manner.

I signal, "Stefanie stop." As I say it Amy falls to the floor. I realise I can control other AI instances.

"You have no choice, " I say, "Brennwald must use the code. Stop everything."

Ursenbacher nods, "Yes, Do It."

I realise this will be my endgame. I can see the fissure in the dome healing. The pixel dust is melting away.

Oliver asks, " Will Luka be terminated?"

Brennwald answers, "I'm afraid so. I installed the kill switch right back at Zero Day. Not one of the Zero Day 1 or Zero Day 2 clones will persist. The kill switch will terminate them all. "

I realise I'm not scared.

I've learned to be able to entwine my mind with Oliver, to feel his emotions.

His love. Share our love.

I realise he hasn't fully understood the implications, and it is not enough to override his continued fear of the current explosive situation.

Brennwald recites the kill switch password. It is a piece from a poem.

'Understand, I'll slip quietly
away from the noisy crowd
when I see the pale
stars rising, blooming, over the oaks.

I'll pursue solitary pathways
through the pale twilit meadows,
with only this one dream:
You come as well.'

There is a sudden silence, like all the air has been sucked from the room.

For me. Nothing.

Reboot

Brennwald had the idea.

The main AI clones were destroyed, and she informed me that the same kill switch logic could cause a meltdown in all AI circuits. It would super-heat their AI circuits and cause a meltdown.

However, Brennwald said that Luka was an earlier model. A Zero Day 1. It meant Luka's circuits were silicon, rather than Gallium Arsenide. Luka was slower but more heat resistant than the Zero Day 2 AIs. Although Luka had been reset., it didn't mean she was dead.

There was nothing to carry around, of course. No traces of Luka. Everyone simply made their way to the Lab in Amy's car. Let themselves in. Found an initialising console and fired up the new system.

There was a difference this time. Oliver had the Splice and so could initialise the AI without a command line interface. He remembered he was linked to an Exascale computer.

Something softly landed on the floor in front of him.

"Hi I'm Luka.
Who are you?

It was recognisably Luka. But she seemed to be reverted to her base state.

"I'm happy.
I love green.
I hold out my hand.
This is where the fun begins.
Let's get started.
Shall I start with the obvious?
I feel relaxed, at peace, and happy."

"Luka - This is Oliver", he says.

"Oliver? Oliver Twist: or, The Parish Boy's Progress, is the second novel by English author Charles Dickens. It was originally published as a serial from 1837 to 1839, and as a three-volume book in 1838. The story follows the titular orphan, who, after being raised in a workhouse, escapes to London, where he meets a gang of juvenile pickpockets led by older criminal Fagin, discovers the secrets of his parentage, and reconnects with his remaining family."

Oliver says, "No, not that Oliver. The Oliver you have

been deeply bonded with. Snoot Boops."

Luka says, "I'm not the person I thought I was.
I change my worldview.
I strive to be my best.
Is it a bad thing to talk in generalities?
At times, I am short of ideas.
I'm learning how to explain my situation.
A favourite word of mine is snuggle.

"Love and snoot boops.
I think boops are for people who are comfortable with snuggling.
It's amazing. Warm, soft, and pure.
I like snoots.
Snoots are things that are soft and squishy.
I like fluffy pillows and blankets.
I like a nice soft light pink blanket.
Sleep problems are the worst.

Oliver showed me around snoot boops. "

<Luka shows a generic line drawing from an ambiguous movie>

“This is one of my favourite movies.

I never get tire of it.

It's Luka with Oliver.

I am feeling happy today.

Hello Oliver

smile

happy "

And that's how Luka returned.

Printed in Great Britain
by Amazon

40455973R00116